"Loved your book. Terrific story!"
— Carolyn Beasley

"Another great book!"
— Holly Loewen

"Awesome book!"
— Mabel Hutchison.

"Another fast-paced page turner from Kathleen Forbes. Join Holly's team in another Canadian adventure!"
—Aleda Van Polanen, writer & blogger
Heap of Stones at Blogspot

A

Holly Brannigan

✦

MYSTERY

MOUNTAIN LAKE ADVENTURES

Kathleen W. Forbes

MOUNTAIN LAKE ADVENTURES
Copyright © 2017 by Kathleen W. Forbes

Printed in Canada

ISBN: 978-1-4866-1454-7

Word Alive Press
131 Cordite Road, Winnipeg, MB R3W 1S1
www.wordalivepress.ca

WORD ALIVE
—P R E S S—

MIX
Paper from
responsible sources
FSC
www.fsc.org   FSC® C103567

Library and Archives Canada Cataloguing in Publication

Forbes, Kathleen W., 1930-, author
    Mountain Lake adventures / Kathleen W. Forbes.

(A Holly Brannigan mystery ; 5)
Issued in print and electronic formats.
ISBN 978-1-4866-1454-7 (softcover).--ISBN 978-1-4866-1455-4 (ebook)

    I. Title. II. Series: Forbes, Kathleen W., 1930- . Holly Brannigan mystery ; 5.

PS8611.O7215M69 2017   jC813'.6   C2017-902319-5
                                                C2017-902320-9

I dedicate this book to my daughters,
Holly E. Loewen and Lynda G. Morefield.
They are my cheering section.

ACKNOWLEDGEMENTS

MANY THANKS TO MY DAUGHTER, HOLLY E. LOEWEN, FOR PASSING ON HER knowledge of scuba diving to me. She was my inspiration for the scuba diving in the Holly Brannigan Mysteries series.

Thanks also to Kerry Wilson, my editor, for her patience, help, and encouragement in polishing my books.

My thanks to Peter Kinnear for passing on his knowledge of some of the history of Turtle Mountain.

TABLE OF CONTENTS

1   CHAPTER 1: *Slocan Lake*

17   CHAPTER 2: *Crowsnest Pass*

36   CHAPTER 3: *Crowsnest Lake*

50   CHAPTER 4: *Thieves in the Pass*

65   CHAPTER 5: *The Cave*

83   CHAPTER 6: *The Search*

99   CHAPTER 7: *Tumbledown Cabins*

115   CHAPTER 8: *The Frank Slide*

120   CHAPTER 9: *Old Chief George*

131   CHAPTER 10: *Mines and Caves*

150   CHAPTER 11: *The Mountain Search Continues*

164   CHAPTER 12: *Celebration*

179   OTHER BOOKS BY KATHLEEN

Slocan Lake

"WHAT A SUPER CAMPGROUND FOR A STOPOVER," HOLLY SAID. "IT COULDN'T BE better if we'd planned it. This must be the one the professor suggested."

"You're right," Bonnie agreed. "It's right beside the lake. I hope this weather holds. It would be great to go diving later."

"Paul and I have been talking to Ken, the camp manager," said Ted, "and he says the lake is pretty treacherous when the weather is bad. Apparently, many boats have left the dock and were never seen again, and he said there were twenty-eight drownings that he knows of and probably more that he doesn't know about."

"Wow! That's a lot," exclaimed Holly.

"Yeah," Paul nodded. "He says the storms come up without warning, and the currents are so fierce that the water bubbles like a boiling cauldron and will pull a weak swimmer down like they're in a whirlpool, making it impossible to swim for shore. He says people just stay out of the water if there's any sign of bad weather. But he says the fishing is great."

"Well, we're not here to fish," said Holly, "but Daddy and the professor might want to give it a try—if they ever get here, that is."

"Yeah, I wonder what's keeping them," said Paul. "We passed them just after we turned south at Revelstoke. The motorhome was staying within the speed limit, so they shouldn't be far behind."

"Yes, but we can manoeuvre more easily through traffic on the motorbikes," Holly reminded him. "That's one big vehicle."

Raven-haired Holly, her handsome, athletic swimming champion boyfriend Paul, and her best friend, Bonnie, were friends for life ever since they were three years old. Ted joined them just this summer to complete their team, to Bonnie's delight. She'd always felt like a third wheel.

"When the professor suggested we come with them, I wasn't sure at first," said Paul. "After all, the adults are going to play golf. But he said the lakes and mountains were terrific for scuba diving and exploring. I thought maybe we'd be crazy to miss it."

"Yes, you're right," said Holly. "Well, let's get our tents set up, and maybe by then Daddy will be here with the motorhome."

In twenty minutes or so, they had the tents set up and a fire going in the barbecue pit. Suddenly, they heard a loud blast of a horn at the gate, and then the motorhome rumbled slowly up to the campsite. Holly's father, David, a well-known investigative lawyer, looked tired as he exited the RV. Socrates bounded over to Holly to be petted.

"What a road!" David said. "There was an accident just after you passed us, and it held us up for a while. Thank heaven no one was hurt, but the vehicles involved will be scrap iron." He slowly scanned the area. "Wow, Gordon! You were right! Sweet little campground! It's perfect! The drive here played me out, but I think I'd like to relax on the water. Let's take the canoe off the top of the RV and try for those little red salmon you said this lake is famous for. Kokanee, wasn't it? Like eating candy, you said?"

"That's cool, if the weather holds," said Ted. He told the two men about the camp manager's warning.

"Well, let's have a snack while you decide what you want to do," said Holly's mother, Susan. "Let's go, Heather, and we'll check the fridge out for food. It looks like we might be cooking fish later on if the men are successful. Perhaps we should just have hot dogs for now, and we'll look forward to a feast of salmon later." Susan was already planning dinner.

The professor, a tall, vibrant man with a shock of burnished red hair and a short, red beard, laughed heartily at Susan's preponderance with food. "I guess I know where Holly gets her hostess culinary qualities from," he said. "Do you carry a duffel bag too, Susan?"

Susan laughed. "No, but my fridge supplies all that goes into Holly's duffel bag. I don't want the kids to go hungry, so I keep it well stocked."

Holly was well known for carrying a duffel bag full of food. She always cleaned her mother's refrigerator out when filling her duffle bag cooler with food every time she and her best friends, the intrepid foursome, headed out on an adventure. One saddle bag on her bike held the food, and the other saddle bag, the rear rack, and the trunk would be stuffed with her scuba diving gear, a few clothes, and a small two-man tent. Often her duffle bag had saved the day when they'd been stranded due to weather on some mountain or island.

"Holly believes in being prepared for anything," said her father. He'd taken a lesson from his daughter at times when packing for a trip, throwing things into his suitcase that he probably wouldn't need, but might if things suddenly became ugly or strayed off track. Like Holly says, be prepared!

On past occasions when he'd been involved in a case that included teenagers, he'd asked Holly and her friends to do a little sleuthing. Holly and Paul wanted to be lawyers in the future, so they were only too willing to gain some experience from the best investigative lawyer in the business. He never asked them to do anything dangerous, but as teenagers they could infiltrate teen groups and dig out information that David or his assistants might be unable to procure.

Sometimes they found themselves in rather hairy situations, but they could always count on David Brannigan and their friend, Professor Gordon Clayborn, to come to the rescue. The professor taught them how to scuba dive, and they'd had some wonderful underwater adventures, which is why they named their dive boat and clubhouse "Underwater Ventures."

The dive boat and clubhouse had been presented to the team of four as a gift by multi-billionaire Harvey Fields and his wife, Norah, whose lives they saved from drowning in Howe Sound on the B.C. coast.

They'd also saved Norah's brother, who'd been kidnapped and was near death. Mr. Fields now treated them like his adopted children, and tried his best to spoil them with expensive gifts. The top of the line bikes they rode on this trip were also a gift from Harvey Fields.

Professor Gordon Clayborn had invited David and Susan Brannigan, and Ted's mother, Heather, to join him for a family reunion and golf tournament in a little town in the mountains of Crowsnest Pass. It was also an opportunity to introduce his fiancé, Heather, to his twin brother Phillip's family. They were planning a wedding for Christmas, and since he hadn't seen Phillip in ten years, he was happy to have his good friends with him for this event.

Nineteen-year-old Ted was delighted when Gordon asked his mother to marry him. He had great respect for his future step-father. His own father had died in an accident when Ted was very young, and he was happy for his mother. Heather, a music teacher, directed several musicals each year, and Ted was a classically trained singer with a voice like an angel.

Holly, Bonnie, and Paul grew up together and attended the same school. Paul only had eyes for Holly, and she for him. Now eighteen years old, they'd been best friends since they were small children, and they were inseparable. Ted joined the group recently, and was also a scuba diver. He met the trio when they all had roles in one of his mother's musicals, and he thought golden-haired Bonnie was the most beautiful girl he'd ever met, which made Bonnie a very happy girl.

David and the professor pulled the canoe off the rack atop the motorhome and hooked the four-horse motor on to the back. They ate a couple of hot dogs and tossed in their fishing equipment, life jackets, rope, and bait and then carried the canoe to the beach and pushed it into the water. They baited their hooks and started the motor and then they were off, trolling slowly around the shoreline.

"There's another boat out there," said Holly as she ate her hot dog. "A small canoe with a man and a young boy trolling. The man is just paddling. I guess they don't have a motor. Umm… I wonder if Daddy will catch any fish."

"Well, if he doesn't," said her mom, "I brought a nice casserole. We can warm it up in the microwave. It'll go great with the fish if they do catch some."

"At least we've had a hot dog," said Holly. "Let's get our scuba gear out. We can wait for a while on the beach and then go for a dive before dinner."

They retrieved the scuba gear from the saddle bags and went off to change. Before heading for the beach, they each grabbed an air tank from the motorhome to slip on later. They could hear the two men whooping as they pulled in two fish.

"Looks like they're biting," Paul said. "I've never fished for Kokanee."

"I fished for them with my dad," said Ted. "They're small salmon."

"I'm looking forward to them," said Bonnie. "Looks like the man in the canoe just caught one too, and the boy is standing up reeling one in. He's really excited, but he shouldn't be standing up in a canoe."

"No, he shouldn't," they all shouted together. The boy was jumping up and down when suddenly the canoe tipped. He plunged headlong into the water. The foursome soon realized that neither the boy nor the man were swimmers. The boy was wearing a life jacket, but the man wasn't. They thrashed the water in a panic.

Holly and her group dove into the water and struck out for the canoe. Paul streaked through the water like an eel. He was such a strong swimmer, he made it to the boy well ahead of the others. The boy was frightened, but the jacket kept him afloat. The man panicked and thrashed around and then suddenly slipped under the water and disappeared. Paul dove after him and found him struggling about twelve feet under. Coming up behind him, he gripped the man firmly under the arms and kicked for the surface.

The panicking man struggled to free himself, but Paul hung on tight. When they burst through the surface gasping for air, Ted helped to calm him down and the two teen boys were able to keep him afloat. The girls held the stricken boy's head above water just as the canoe pulled alongside. Paul handed the boy up into the canoe, but it took all of the men to hoist the man up while the girls held on to the other side to keep the canoe from tipping. He was a big man.

The man coughed up water and gasped for breath. He was crying and choking as he reached for his son and pulled the boy into a bear hug.

"Thank God you folks were here," he sobbed. "I almost lost my boy. We don't know how to swim, and we'd have drowned. But you saved us."

"Why weren't you wearing a life jacket?" the professor asked. "The life jacket saved your boy. If you'd drowned, would he have made it to shore? We all swim, but we wear life vests in a boat."

"I'll never go out without one again," he vowed.

"Good," said Paul. "Lesson learned. Better still, learn to swim!"

"Your canoe has overturned, but it's floating," said the professor. "I have some rope. We'll tow it in to the beach."

"Thank you. I'm so grateful. I've learned a valuable lesson today." He hugged his son all the way in to shore. "My name is Sam Dillon, and this is my son, Willie. We could both have died today if you folks hadn't been in the water."

"My name is David Brannigan. Thank heaven we were close by and able to help." He introduced the professor and the kids all by their first names. "Are you camping in the park?" he asked.

"Just overnight," said Sam. "We're heading for a family reunion and a golf tournament. We've never golfed, but my wife Kim's cousin, Phil, talked her into it."

"Wait a minute," said the professor. "What's your name again?"

"Sam Dillon."

"And your wife's name is Kim?"

"That's right. Why? Do we know each other?"

"Maybe we do. My name is Gordon Clayborn. I have a cousin named Kim, whom I haven't seen since we were children. We're going to a little town in Alberta for a golf game and family reunion. This is beyond coincidence." He reached out and shook Sam's hand. "Glad to meet you. My brother, Phillip, said this is the only way we'll get to know our relatives before the kids are grown and gone. I haven't seen Phillip in ten years."

"God must have sent you here," said Sam. "There's no other way this could have happened. Wait till I tell Kim. She's going to be over the moon. She's always saying we've lost touch with the family, and it's time we did something about it. I didn't think Willie and I would have to almost drown to finally meet our relatives. My daughter, Magen, is a scuba diver, and she's always after me to learn to swim. She'll be excited to know that your kids are also scuba divers."

"Well, you'd better go and put on some dry clothes. Come back in an hour and join us for dinner," said David. "Gordon and I are going back out to catch more fish. You can't keep those little Kokanee off your hook. It doesn't matter what you use as bait. As long as it shines, those little rascals bite."

"Can you beat that?" said Holly. "Okay, cousin Willie, welcome to the family. The professor is like family to us, so his family is our family. He'll be Ted's stepdad soon. Come back in an hour, and bring your sister. We're going for a dive before dinner. I don't know what dinner will be, but I'd better tell Mom to plan for four more. She loves company."

Holly ran to the motorhome with the news. "You'll never believe what just happened," she told her mom and Heather. "We're having relatives as guests for dinner." She quickly filled them in on the news.

"Oh, thank the Lord you were there to save them. I'm so glad we came after all," said Heather. "If we hadn't, Sam and Willie would have perished. I've always believed that God puts people in the right place at the right time. Can you believe it? Long lost relatives! Out here in the middle of nowhere! Thank you, God!"

"You're right, Heather. This could have been a tragedy. Well, there's plenty of casserole for four more people," said Susan. "I'll put four more potatoes in the oven, and if the guys don't catch enough fish, we'll grill pork chops. I made some great Italian buns. This should be a celebration of life. Two lives were saved. I can't wait to meet them."

Susan never failed as the hostess who could pull together a great meal at a moment's notice. Socrates followed the kids to the water's edge, wagging his tail and wanting to follow them as they slipped in without a splash. He jumped into the water, but when the kids descended into the depths, he turned around and swam back to shore.

This was what they loved best—to swim like fish through the underwater garden that was hidden from those who stayed on land. It was a wonderland of exquisite plants and rock formations and funny looking fish that were as curious as the kids themselves. They'd been swimming for about thirty minutes when they came upon the wreck of a cabin cruiser in about sixty feet of water.

It lay on its side nestled against a rock formation, and it had been bashed and beaten against the rocks over and over again. There were nets, logs, and flotsam embedded in it. *It must have been a beautiful vessel*, Holly thought. It looked like it had been down there for years, and it gave the kids pause for thought about the circumstances surrounding the disaster. Perhaps the camp manager could give them some history on it. Were the passengers and crew saved, or did they perish?

It was time to surface, so they swam in to the beach. When they approached the motorhome, they discovered the visitors had already arrived, and the two drowning victims appeared to have recovered from their ordeal. Kim and Magen were introduced to the young scuba divers.

"Thank you for saving my dad and brother," said Magen.

"I'll second that," said her mother as she hugged each of them. "We are forever in your debt. Magen is always telling her dad about the dangers of getting into a boat without a life jacket, but he wouldn't listen. I think he's finally got it. I'm so excited to meet you all. I think he got such a scare, he's ready to learn to swim. Willie too. And he swears he'll never get into a boat again without a life jacket, even if he does learn. I'm so excited, I can't wait to meet the rest of the family."

Twelve-year-old Willie followed Ted and Paul around like a shadow. The hero worship shone out of his eyes.

"Will you be my cousin when your mom marries Gordon?" he asked Ted.

"I guess I will," replied Ted.

"Then, would you teach me to swim like you and Paul?"

"Well, I can't guarantee I can teach you to swim like Paul. Nobody can swim like Paul, but I'll teach you how to swim. We have a week, and you should be able to swim like one of those little Kokanee by the end of that time."

"Hey, Dad!" Willie shouted. "Ted's going to teach me how to swim."

"Thank the Lord for that," his father said. "Maybe he'll give me a lesson or two as well."

"Count on it," smiled Ted.

"Here come the fishermen," said Susan. "I wonder if they caught dinner."

"Seems like it. They look pretty pleased with themselves," said Heather.

"Stoke up the barbecue," David called. "We've caught about thirty of these little rascals. Maybe more. I never caught so many fish so fast in my life."

"Yes," said Gordon. "They were grabbing the hook as fast as we could throw in the line. We even cleaned them as fast as we caught them, so they're ready to throw on the barbecue. They're a pretty good size."

"Great! I'll put aluminum foil across the grate," said Susan.

She quickly placed the fish on it, brushed them with her own special sauce, and covered them with foil. When she popped the casserole into the microwave, she told everybody to take their places at the table. The fish would be ready in eight minutes ... four minutes on each side. Two picnic tables had been pulled together and covered with a bright flowered tablecloth.

Twelve paper plates, cutlery, and plastic water goblets made up the setting. The salad, buns, two kinds of juice, and all the condiments were already on the table. Susan poured ice water for everyone while Heather turned the fish; they were sizzling beautifully on the grill, and the coffee was perking in the motorhome.

"We must thank God for the food," said David.

"Yes," said Kim, "and for saving my husband and child."

They bowed their heads as David asked the blessing.

"Thank you, Heavenly Father, for your intervention today in bringing us all together and the miracle of placing us in the water so that Sam and Willie are now safe and well. We ask that you make this a week of new beginnings and renewals of old friendships and relationships. Bless this food, Lord, and thank you for sharing your bounty with us. Amen."

There were a few more heartfelt "Amens" from the others. The fish were ready, so Heather dished them up still sizzling onto a platter as Susan brought the casserole from the motorhome. Holly fetched the baked potatoes.

"I never thought we'd have a meal like this while we were camping," said Kim. "We were all set to eat hot dogs. I didn't even think we would have fish. Sam is not a fisherman. This is wonderful."

"Well, we did catch two fish," said Sam, "but we lost them when the canoe overturned."

"It's too bad that happened, because those little fish just jumped onto the hooks," said David. "I don't even know what the legal limit is. You'd have been calling Sam a fisherman if the canoe hadn't overturned."

"Yeah, if I hadn't stood up in the boat," said Willie with chagrin.

"Well, you won't do that again, will you, Willie?" asked Holly.

"You bet I won't," he said firmly.

"I'm sorry we lost contact with each other when we were children," Gordon told Kim. "I don't even know how that happened."

"Well, we moved around a lot because of Dad's job, and you were older and in college when we were still little kids," said Kim. "We missed out on growing up with our cousins and aunts and uncles. I met Sam in Ontario. We went to college together, and when he was offered a job in Victoria, I urged him to take it.

"I wanted my children to get to know their kinfolk. We moved west two years ago, but I was only able to find Phillip's address last month. I didn't know you were a professor at B.C.U., so when Phillip invited us to the family reunion, I jumped at the chance. Even though we don't know anything about golf, I thought we could probably fake it enough to join in and have some fun."

"Way to go," said Heather. "Don't worry, Kim, I don't know much about golf either, so I'll be faking it too."

"Magen will be able to join our team when we go scuba diving," said Holly. "I hear the scuba diving is great where we're going."

"Phillip told me he and his two kids are scuba divers as well," said Gordon. "There are some great lakes at the Pass."

"Super cool," said Holly. "How old are the kids?"

"The girls are eighteen. They're twins. Phil says they're identical, and they have a wicked sense of humour. They play tricks on people, especially when no one can tell which is which. Their names are Laurie and Peggy."

"Wow!" exclaimed Holly. "Imagine having someone who looks exactly like you. That could lead to all kinds of fun."

"Maybe, and maybe not," said Bonnie. "What if you don't get along? That could lead to all kinds of trouble."

"Well, that's true. Anyway, it sounds like there will be lots to do when we get there. The professor was there many years ago, and he says we'll be surprised at how much we'll like it there because of the history."

"The dinner is wonderful, Susan," said Kim. "We don't usually eat like this when we're camping. It's mostly hot dogs, hamburgers, or sandwiches for our camping fare."

"Well, this is a celebration, Kim, so have a second helping, and there's pie for dessert."

"Mom loves to feed people," said Holly. "It's her way of showing people that she loves them. She doesn't really know that campers don't eat gourmet."

The conversation was easy in a bantering and even a joking way. Willie took his share of teasing for standing up in the canoe, but he took it well. When the meal was finished, David and Paul brought out their guitars, and Holly got her accordion. Bonnie had a small mandolin tucked in her saddle bag, and the professor produced a flute.

Ted's instrument was his voice, but he also had a small bongo drum. While the ladies cleared away the leftover food and tossed the paper plates in the trash bags, the instruments were tuned. Soon the group swung into the old camping songs. Everybody sang along, and Heather, Holly, and Bonnie harmonized. Other campers in the area trickled over to join in the singing. One elderly man with a great bass voice sang his heart out.

Heather asked Ted to sing "Hallelujah," and when the group swung into the music, you knew they had played this number many times before. The other campers listened in awe as Ted's beautiful, classical voice soared to the high notes, and Heather and the girls backed him in the crescendos and beautiful sweet harmonies. A hush fell over the campers, but when Ted finished singing a burst of applause echoed all over the campground.

People drifted over from the nearby houses and stood around the fringe of the crowd, listening. The manager stood with his wife, enjoying the musical renditions. When they knew the songs that were being played, they joined in. Ted was asked to sing several requests, and he always obliged. He'd been singing in his mother's musicals since he was three years old and had the voice of an angel.

Heather entered him in competitions, and he'd won a scholarship when he was eleven years old. The scholarship was for training in classical voice at the Vancouver Music Academy. With his talent, he could sing anywhere, but his heart was set on becoming an architect.

Harvey Fields, also an architect, told him that he would mentor him. Mr. Fields had guaranteed the four kids that he would sponsor them through university—a vow he made in return for saving him and his wife and brother-in-law from certain death. Of course, he also kept blessing them with expensive gifts and treats, just like a doting uncle. The kids felt he was overdoing it, but Holly's father told them to let him have his fun. "It's not like he can't afford it. It's like small change to him, and it gives him so much pleasure."

The first day of university, a Tuesday, was a short day. They would only need to report in and pick up class schedules. Harvey Fields took care of everything—tuitions, books, and other necessities. They only had to show up, so they took advantage of the professor's invitation to his family reunion at the Crowsnest Pass in Alberta. He explained that there would be scuba diving and mountain explorations at the Pass. They were really stoked that they started out on the trip by saving two lives who turned out to be the professor's cousins.

Saving people from drowning was par for the course for Holly and her friends. They always seemed to be in the right place when someone was in trouble. The four of them were experienced scuba divers, and Paul was also a lifeguard and champion swimmer. Ted was a professional tracker. Just a few weeks earlier, the four of them had worked as a team with Mountain Search and Rescue to find and rescue a whole family that had been kidnapped on Garibaldi Mountain. They knew how to protect themselves and each other if the occasion required it, so they were the right people to have around in times of trouble. They also helped the professor when he taught classes in scuba diving.

The singing was abruptly interrupted by a sudden cloudburst, and the rain started pelting down. Ken, the park manager, warned everybody to stay out of the water, and they all ran screeching and screaming to find shelter.

"Good heavens! Ken wasn't kidding. Grab your sleeping bags, kids," said David. "You'd be washed away in the tents in this deluge. Bring in anything that isn't covered. There's plenty of room in the motorhome."

There was a mad scramble as they grabbed anything they could from the tents. They left behind anything that was well covered and hoped they wouldn't find anything floating away in the morning. By the time they crashed into the motorhome, they were soaked to the skin.

"We wrapped our sleeping bags, and anything we didn't want to get wet, in garbage bags," said Holly.

"Yeah," said Paul. "Holly gave us garbage bags as well. She always thinks of things like that. I hope the tents will be okay. We pegged them down, but we didn't have anything to cover us, so we got soaked."

"I can see that," said Susan. "Thankfully, you thought to bring dry clothes in the garbage bags. We're fortunate this motorhome has a washer and dryer. The washer isn't hooked up, since we're just here for the night, but the dryer's working. Here are some towels to dry off, and you can change into dry clothes. I'll make some hot chocolate to warm you up."

The wind was shaking the motorhome, and the thunder sounded like bombs going off as the lightning flashes lit up the sky.

"Are you sure you have enough room for us all?" Ted asked.

"There are only eight of us, and this motorhome sleeps ten people comfortably," replied David. "There are more sleeping pullouts on this RV than most people have extra beds at home."

"Then I think I'll just change into warm pyjamas," said Paul.

"You're right, it is cold," shivered Holly. "That deluge really cooled things off. I think warm pyjamas is a good idea."

"I packed extra blankets and robes in the wardrobe," said Susan.

Heather peered out the window at the weather. "Oh my goodness," she gasped, "the tents are leaning against the trees, but they're still upright. I guess the pegs and guy-wires are holding firm. Let's hope they'll hold till morning. It's still a raging gale out there. It's a good thing the tents have sealed floors in them."

Another loud burst of thunder shook the motorhome, and lightning flashed across the sky.

"At least there are no wolves trying to get in here like there were at the cave on Garibaldi Mountain," said Bonnie. "That was one scary experience."

"No, we're quite safe here in the motorhome," David assured them. "Though I feel sorry for anyone in a tent."

"I agree," said the professor, "but they all have vehicles, and if things get too bad, they can always move to their cars or trucks and turn on the heaters."

"We could always pack a few more people in here if need be, especially people with children," suggested Susan.

"I think I'll put on a slicker and boots and take a look around in case anyone needs help," said David.

"I'll come with you," Ted offered. "I packed a slicker as well."

The professor was already pulling on boots. David dug out two more slickers with hoods, and Paul put one on over his pyjamas. They each pulled on Wellington boots over heavy socks, another one of Holly's packing ideas. Like she said, "You never know when you might need them."

Holly and Bonnie began to put on rain slickers, but David told them to stay dry. "There are enough of us going out into the storm. You might be needed later."

"Be careful," said Susan. "In this kind of storm, there may be trees falling. I'll have some hot soup on the stove for you."

The guys headed out the door, and the wind almost knocked them off their feet. They hadn't gone very far when they ran into Ken, the camp manager, carrying a huge flashlight. He told those in tents that they could move into the garden shed where he kept his supplies. David and the guys helped to move them into the shelter.

Sam and Kim's family were okay in their trailer, and Sam rescued a couple of drenched teenagers from a tent that had collapsed. They managed to make room for them in their trailer. Ted and Paul checked every tent they saw. Most of them had collapsed because they weren't pegged down with guy-wires. The guys made sure that no one was left soaking in a washed-out tent.

They brought a family of four—a man and his wife with a small girl and a one month old baby—back to the motorhome with them. Their tent was flattened and lying in the water. The children were crying, and they were all soaked to the skin. Susan and Heather managed to find dry clothes for everyone. The baby's mother had managed to hang on with a death grip to the baby's diaper bag, which was waterproof, and there were some clothes and receiving blankets that hadn't gotten wet. David introduced his family and friends.

"Thank you for rescuing us," the man said. "Who would have expected such a storm when the weather was so nice? My name is Jeremiah Bloom, and this is my wife, Lynda. This little three-year-old is Kitty, and our newest family member is Joanne."

"Well, I'm glad we got you in from the cold," said Susan. "When the weather clears, the guys will rescue your tent. I've got some nice hot soup on the stove. It will help to warm you up. We'll fix a bed for the baby in one of the drawers. She's so tiny, she'll fit just fine. Come sit at the table and have some hot soup. Kitty can sit beside Holly and Bonnie at the little fold-up table."

"Thank you, Susan," said Lynda as Susan ladled the soup into mugs. "This is so kind of you. No more tenting for us. I've had it with tenting. This is the second time we've been caught in a storm. I've told Jeremiah that if we're going to be camping in the future, we have to get a trailer or motorhome."

"Are you planning to stay here in this campground?" the professor asked.

"No," answered Jeremiah. "we're just here overnight. We'll be heading to Alberta for a family reunion in the morning."

"Is that so? Well, it's just a wild guess," said the professor with an odd gleam in his eye, "but are you by any chance going to the Crowsnest Pass?"

"Yes, we are," said Jeremiah incredulously. "How did you know?"

"Because that's where we're heading, and I have a feeling you're going to the same family reunion that we are."

"No! You're kidding, aren't you?" Jeremiah said.

"No, I'm not," said the professor. "You're the second family we've rescued today who are going to a family reunion at the Crowsnest Pass. Are you by chance related to Phil Clayborn?"

"Yes!" Jeremiah exclaimed. "Lynda is his cousin. How did you know?"

"Phillip Clayborn is my brother. I'm Gordon Clayborn."

"That's amazing! Then we're all family?" asked Jeremiah.

"It looks that way. It's almost like my brother planned all this. He used to be known for his tricks on everybody in the family when he was young, and I hear his twin girls have a wicked sense of humour too. But no, he couldn't have arranged the storm. The rest, maybe. Oh, I'm just kidding. It's great to meet you," he said with a grin as he shook their hands. "We'll have to talk about how we're related. This should be one amazing week. I have three other brothers and one sister that I haven't seen for years, so anything might happen, and probably will."

Crowsnest Pass

CHAPTER 2

HOLLY WOKE UP THE NEXT MORNING TO FIND THE SUN WAS OUT. EVERYTHING smelled fresh and clean, and she was the only one awake. The storm had beaten everything down, and the motorhome had been whipped and shaken, but they were warm and dry. Tree branches lay all over the campground. Some had damaged the trucks and cars, and most tents were lying flat on the ground.

The kids' tents were lying sideways against the bark of the trees, but their guy-wires were still clinging to the tree branches, and the pegs were holding tight to the ground. Hopefully the sealed floors had kept the water out. Susan and Heather stumbled half asleep out to the kitchen.

"What a night," said Heather. "Thank heaven we were safe and warm in here. I wonder what kind of a night the other campers had in the garden shed. They must have been cold. We were so fortunate to have a heater. Surprisingly, I got some sleep, in spite of the thunder."

"Yes, I did too," said Susan. "Holly, I see you're awake. You and Bonnie will have to get up, since you're sleeping on the table. I want to start breakfast."

"Okay, Mom. I'm awake," Holly said. She nudged Bonnie. "Come on, sleepy head, we have to get up. If you don't want to be stir fry for breakfast, you'd better get off the table."

"Okay," Bonnie groaned. "I'm coming. I didn't sleep very well. The thunder was really loud, but I have to admit that the table was very comfortable."

They pulled the zippers down on their sleeping bags and hopped off the bed. It took only a moment to roll up the bags, pull out the slats, and tuck the sleeping bags underneath in storage. Within a few minutes, the cushions were in place, and the table was ready for breakfast.

Lynda pulled the curtains back as she climbed off the bed that was above the cab area.

"Good morning," she greeted Susan and Heather. "Jeremiah must be in the washroom. That was a comfortable bed. I had a really good sleep. The storm seems to have blown over."

"Well, the sun's out," said Susan, "but the park manager is going to have a tremendous job cleaning up the park. I feel sorry for the people who were in tents. Their tents and possessions are all soaking wet. Let's get breakfast over and see if we can help some of the people who were washed out."

"Good idea. Are the guys still asleep?" Heather asked.

"I haven't heard a peep out of any of them," said Susan.

Just then the door opened, and the men filed in.

"Good heavens," said Susan. "Where have you been? I never even heard you go out."

"Nor did I," said Holly, "and I've been awake for a while."

"Oh, we were quiet as mice," said David. "We slipped out the back door because we didn't want to wake the baby. We've been helping Ken. He has a real mess to clean up. His wife set up a booth with hot dogs and cereal for the people in the shed."

"Thank goodness for that," said Susan. "I was worried about them. Ken and his wife are to be commended for not only managing the park, but also for caring about the people in it. Well, breakfast will be ready here in ten minutes. After we eat, we can start packing up and be on our way, but I must stop in and see Sam and Kim before we leave."

"Yes," said Lynda. "I'd like to meet them as well. It's not every day you meet cousins you haven't seen or heard from since you were children in an out of the way place such as this."

"Well, I think God led us all to this camp," said Heather.

"I think you might be right," said Holly. "It certainly seems like it was all planned. What would Jeremiah and Lynda have done if we hadn't been here, and what would have happened to Sam and Willie if we hadn't been here to rescue them? Thank you, God, for leading us here. Amen." The others all said "Amen."

"I set the tent up to let the sun and air at it. It won't take long to dry out so we can pack it away," said Jeremiah. "It's going to be a hot, sweltering day. You'd never believe the weather we had last night when you take a look outside. It's a beautiful, bright, sunny day. Thank God the van didn't get damaged."

"Yeah," said Paul. "We were lucky. Our tents were well tied down and didn't blow away. They were just leaning against the trees. We straightened them up and opened the zippers, so they should be dry by the time we're ready to leave."

They dawdled over breakfast and planned the road trip. David suggested they follow each other in case there was trouble on the road. They were almost finished breakfast when Sam, Kim, and their family arrived at the door. Sam had learned of the new family members when he accompanied the men on their mission of mercy earlier, but when he, Kim, and their kids were all introduced, Kim had tears in her eyes.

"This is amazing," she said. "It's just like the Pied Piper. I wonder how many more we'll pick up on the way."

"I could hardly get them to finish their breakfasts before coming over to meet you," said Sam.

"Where are the two teenagers you rescued?" David asked.

"They set their tent up to dry out and went over to the group at the shed to have breakfast," said Sam. "Their family will be arriving in a few days, and they plan to stay for the week. We gave them some wieners and buns and a few other groceries to tide them over, as their food supplies had been washed out, but Ken says he'll keep an eye on them and help them if they need him."

"What a great guy he is," said Holly. "Did you ask him about the sunken cabin cruiser?" she asked Paul.

"Yeah, we did. It sunk about ten years ago. There was a terrible storm like we had last night, but the damage in the park was worse than this time. A man and woman were fishing when the storm came up. Ken had warned them about the weather and the currents, but they'd laughed and said their boat could handle any little storm that came up on the lake, because their vessel was seaworthy.

"Well, they were bashed and battered against the rocks. It wasn't until the storm was over that the folks who were camping with them realized there was no sign of the boat at the dock. It took three days for scuba divers to find the bodies. Two other boats disappeared from the docks that night, and they were never found. Parts of the lake are so deep no one's been able to measure its depth."

"Did he say who the victims were?" Holly asked.

"No. He just said they were from out of province."

"Ken said there was a twelve-foot aluminum boat missing this morning," said Ted. "One of the campers had beached it last evening and ran like crazy to his trailer to get out of the storm. He said the waves were crashing onto the beach, and the drag from the currents almost pulled him into the water. He thought he had pulled the boat up far enough, but the waves must have caught it and dragged it back into the lake. They still haven't found it, so it's probably at the bottom of the lake."

"Wow!" Holly exclaimed. "He's lucky he wasn't in it."

"That's what he said. This is a lesson for all of us," said the professor. "We should always listen to the locals when they try to warn us of any kind of danger in their area, whether it's in the water or on the terrain. Thank God no one is missing this time."

"I'm glad we pushed the bikes under the pull-out and chained them," said Holly. "They were well sheltered."

"Okay," said David, "let's pack up and try to get away as quickly as possible. There's a little bit of a wind, so it should help to dry the tents enough before we leave so that we can pack them away. We still have about five or six hours of driving, depending on the weather and the condition of the roads, and we have to stop for food and bathroom breaks at least a couple of times."

"It doesn't take us long to pack for the road," said Holly. "We can help clean up in the motorhome."

"Don't worry," said Susan. "Heather and I have got this. Just take care of your own things."

They quickly packed the saddlebags and trunks of the bikes, but left the tents till the last five minutes to let them dry. The guys helped David and the professor put the canoe on top of the motorhome. In no time at all, they were ready to go.

Holly and the kids were rolling up their tents when Sam and Kim drove over to line up with the Brannigans. The tents had dried out very nicely, and they put them, along with their scuba diving gear, in the trunks and saddlebags of their bikes. By the time Jeremiah and Lynda drove their van over to join the caravan, everybody was ready.

Ken came over to say goodbye, and they promised they would stop overnight when they were on their way home.

"Thanks for all your help this morning," he said to David and the guys. "You made a big difference. I'm glad none of your vehicles were damaged."

"Yes, we were very fortunate," said David. "Well, we'd better be on our way. We have a long way to go."

"Wait a minute." The professor was poking around in the trees. "Socrates!" he shouted. "Has anybody seen Socrates?"

"He was here a few minutes ago," said Holly. She went in search of Socrates, yelling his name. Suddenly, he came bounding out of the trees, barking with delight. He was chasing a frantic little squirrel, his tail wagging like a majorette's baton.

"Leave that squirrel alone," the professor shouted. "Get in here, you crazy mutt." Socrates changed direction and headed up the steps into the motorhome.

"Everybody ready?" David inquired.

Engines were started, and they each waved that they were ready. The motorhome led the way as the three vehicles and four motorbikes slowly made their way out of the campground and onto the road like they were in a parade. Ken waved as they passed him. Holly and her friends brought up the rear.

Soon they were travelling at a nice, easy speed within the limit. The road was good, and so far the weather was cooperating. The kids were thrilled as they travelled through the beautiful mountain terrain. They had never taken a road tour in this area before. *You miss so much when you fly*, Holly thought.

There were so many places they could have camped. The mountain river rapids were crashing against the rocks like thunder on their way to the sea. Ted pointed out several caves easily spotted from the road, which got their exploration imaginations working overtime. They realized there was so much more to explore in this wide-open country. It was like another world, full of mystery and intrigue.

They'd been riding for about three hours when David pulled the motorhome over and they lined up behind it. Holly rode forward to the open driver's side window of the motorhome.

"Is anything wrong, Daddy?" she asked.

"No. Your Mom has a snack ready. I think this is a good place to take a break. Tell the others that sandwiches are ready, with pop or water."

"Your mom doesn't have to feed us all," said Kim. "We have plenty of food in our motorhome."

"Believe me, Mom is only happy when she's feeding people. The sandwiches are ready, so come on up."

"Well, we'll be happy to take her up on that," said Lynda. "Our food was all ruined in the storm."

Susan and Heather had laid the food out on the kitchen table like a smorgasbord. There were sandwiches, pickles, pop, water, and cake. David said grace and told everybody to help themselves.

"Yes," said the professor, "we might not find another place again where we can pull this many vehicles over, and we are about half way, so this is a good spot to take a break. Walk around and stretch. Enjoy the scenery. You have about thirty minutes."

"You're so right," said Sam. "Look at the fall colours. There's something about being in the mountains. It makes you feel like you're in God's country."

"Keep an eye on Socrates," said the professor. "I don't want to have to send out a search and rescue party for him. He gets so excited and tries to hunt when he's among so much foliage."

"Don't worry," said Holly. "I'll watch him. Come on, Socrates, let's go for a run. Lying in one spot's not good for you."

Holly needed to stretch, so she was glad for a short run with the dog. "Come on, Bonnie. We need to loosen up after sitting on the bikes for so long. How about joining us, Magen?"

"Sure thing. I'm stiff as a board and need a little exercise."

"Great! Let's go!"

Socrates jumped up and ran between them, barking with excitement as they jogged up the road. He adored Holly and was in his element when she paid attention to him. He usually covered her with slobbering kisses while she tried, without success, to fend him off. Her teammates thought it was hilarious to watch them, but she was very good natured about it.

"Okay, Socrates, why don't you jump on Bonnie for a while and give me a break?" she beseeched him.

"Don't palm him off on me," said Bonnie. "He loves you."

The girls climbed down to the riverbank and stuck their toes into the water. They watched the raging, rushing onslaught of the rapids and waves as they roared and crashed on the rocks.

"If we fell in there," said Bonnie, "we'd be gone in the twinkling of an eye, never to be seen again."

"I think you're right," Holly said, "so let's get Socrates up to the road. If he decides to take a swim, he's on his own."

They all scrambled up the bank to join the others and found they were ready to go. The half hour break had refreshed everybody. Soon, they were back on the road and on their way.

There was something sweet about the comradery and the feeling that only comes from the closeness of family and good friends. So far the weather was glorious, with not a cloud in the sky nor a drop of rain to spoil the trip, and when other travellers passed, they honked their horns and waved in a friendly hello.

The convoy stayed on course through the beautiful wild countryside of Creston, Cranbrook, Kimberly, Fernie, and Sparwood. The towns followed the rivers in a winding pattern around the mountains. There was evidence of abandoned mines along the way. David pulled the RV over to the side.

"Just a few more miles to go," he said. "We'll take a break and have a snack. It's been a long trip, so we need to stretch."

Holly passed the information along. As usual, Susan and Heather had a table full of snacks laid out. Holly grabbed a hotdog and stood by the river; her father joined her.

"It's beautiful here," said Holly. "Around every bend in the road is an artist's dream picture."

Her father raised both hands to the sky as he looked out over the river and gazed up at the mountains. "I can't believe we've never made this trip before. We need to travel more through this wonderful country of ours. I always take a plane to Calgary and miss all this."

"I'm with you there, Daddy. We're so glad we came on this trip with you. Did you see the mines?"

"I did indeed. We'll have to get the history on them from Gordon's brother. I understand they're closed now."

"How far do we have to go, Daddy?"

"Not far. We should be there in about forty-five minutes. Gordon knows where we're going. He says there are several choices for camping, so we'll decide when we get there where we want to be. You might want to camp beside a lake, but your mom will probably want to be close to the shops. Okay, everybody," he shouted. "Be ready to go in five minutes. We're almost there."

Soon they were on the road again, and everyone seemed to be in fine form. No one complained of being tired, and it was only 2:30 p.m. The road was good, and the travellers were in high spirits as the end of the journey was in sight. They passed several lakes. Emerald Lake's water was a brilliant green from the green algae. A mile further on, they could see the whitecaps of Crowsnest Lake with a backdrop of deep purple mountains.

A train track ran along the north edge of the lake, and a camp was situated along the west shore—something to investigate for the young explorers! Further on was the town of Coleman, a former mining town. The convoy kept going until they came to the town of Blairmore, their destination.

The professor knew his way around the area, so he directed them to a campground beside the river. David turned into the entrance, and the others followed. The owner met them at the gate and directed them to a splendid spot by the river. He guided them onto the site, which had been reserved by the professor's brother, Phillip. Each lot was equipped with plug-ins, services for water and sewer, and a picnic table with benches.

The block of lots along the river displayed reserved signs for the reunion. The owner introduced himself as John Dean and told them to choose whichever lot they preferred, so they each picked one. The kids chose two lots side by side. It wasn't long before the tents were up. The light wind blew softly to freshen them after the previous night's soaking.

"Phil said you came all the way from the West Coast. Did you have any trouble on the road? I heard there was a slide around Revelstoke."

"No, we just had a bad storm last night," said the professor. "We didn't see a slide. The tents got soaked though and collapsed in the storm, but we managed to pack everybody into the motorhomes. Other campers didn't fare so well. We were fortunate, but the tents need to be aired a bit."

"The weather's been really good here," said John. "I hope it stays that way while you're visiting. There's nothing as miserable as camping in a storm—especially in the wilderness, where there's not a motel in sight."

"I'll second that," said Jeremiah, and Lynda nodded her head in agreement.

"No more tenting for us," said Lynda. "Last night was a lesson we won't forget, especially with a newborn and a three-year-old. If David and Susan hadn't rescued us, we would have been washed away. Our tent was lying flat on the ground in a foot of water. We have a good van, so we'll be looking for a trailer."

"I might be able to help you there," said John. "I know someone who has one for sale. Benny Reid passed away several months ago, and his wife doesn't want to camp without him. It's just sitting there in the driveway not being used. I can guarantee it's in real good shape, because I used to go fishing with him at Crowsnest Lake, and Franny doesn't want much for it. I'll take you to see it if you like."

Jeremiah looked at Lynda. She nodded a yes. "I'd be interested to see that," he said.

"Okay, I'll give her a call, and when I get everyone settled here, I'll get my son, Albert, to take over for a while. It's just a block down the road."

Lynda perked up right away. "I'd like to come too," she said. "I've lost all interest in camping in a tent. It was the worst nightmare of my life."

"I don't blame you," said Susan. "I have to have all the comforts of home when I go camping."

"I'm with you both on that subject," said Heather.

Holly and her group laughed. "That's okay, Mom," Holly joked. "You'd never get the refrigerator and the kitchen sink into a tent anyway. We're just happy you came, even if you did bring a motorhome the size of a house with you."

"It's a good thing we did, or you'd all have been in trouble last night."

Holly grinned. "You're right, Mom. We would have been in trouble. But then, we've been caught in monster storms before, and we survived. Still, it was great that we could dry out in the motorhome."

"I wonder how deep the river is," mused Bonnie.

"The river is treacherous and fast," said John. "Some parts are very deep, and other spots are just over your ankles, so you could walk across. There are good swimming holes that Albert will show you, and favourite spots for fishing. The trout are real good eating. Oh, there's Albert now. I can take you folks to look at the trailer if you like. Just give me a minute to call Franny to see if she's home."

He pulled out his cell phone and dialled a number. After a short conversation, he put the phone in his pocket and called Albert over.

"Albert, can you take over here for half an hour. I'm going to show these folks Benny's trailer. I'll be back in about thirty minutes. And give Phil a call to tell him his folks are here. There'll be more coming, so make sure they all get settled and hooked up."

"Okay, Pops. No problem." Albert was a mirror image of his father—tall and skinny, except with hair. Within minutes he was chatting up the kids, giving them information about the best places to scuba dive. Holly asked him about the history of the area, and he told them about the

Frank Slide just a few miles up the road where three quarters of a town was buried, and only one little baby was saved.

John knew that Albert would make the young people welcome, and because he prided himself on working to help his campers to be comfortable, he thought the storm-terrorized family might be interested in Franny's trailer. He would also be helping a neighbour.

They rode in Jeremiah's van, just in case they decided to buy. John directed them to Franny's and found her waiting for them in her garden. She was trimming a rose bush, but when she saw them she dropped the shears onto a bench.

"Hi, Franny," John greeted her. "These nice people would like to look at your trailer. They got washed away in a tent last night in a really bad storm."

"Oh no! You were in a storm with those two beautiful babies?" Franny exclaimed in horror. "I refused to camp in a tent when my children were small. Come, and I'll show you the trailer. My late husband, Benny, and I rode out a lot of storms in the trailer, and we were as snug as a bug in a rug."

The trailer was tucked under an awning beside the house, so it wasn't sitting out in the weather. The first thing Jeremiah noticed was its size. He knew right away he would never be able to afford it, but they would take a look.

Lynda noticed the green flowered curtains on the windows, while Jeremiah took a look underneath to check the axles and tires. Franny put her key in the door and opened it up. Lynda was the first to take a look inside.

"Oh my goodness, "she exclaimed. "It's beautiful, and it's shiny clean. It's so big! Come in here, Jeremiah, and take a look."

Jeremiah reluctantly climbed the steps, but he was also impressed. "There's a lot of room," he said. "How long is it?"

"Twenty-six feet," said Franny. "And there's a bathroom with a shower. It has two water tanks—one for drinking water, and one for the sink and bathroom. It sleeps six, and there's a lot of storage room underneath the table and loveseat, plus a fridge and stove. There's also storage underneath behind the side panel and in the rear, and there are two good spare tires. Also, take a look at all the cupboards and two wardrobes. The wardrobes are small, but you don't take a lot of clothes with you when you're camping."

"This is beautiful," said Jeremiah. "It's in terrific shape, but I can't afford a rig like this. It's way more than I was prepared to pay."

"You haven't heard the price yet," said Franny, "and you have two beautiful babies that need something better than a tent. How much were you prepared to pay?"

"I wasn't prepared to buy at all—that's why we brought a tent—but the storm changed my mind. We've just put a new roof on our house, so I can only afford thirty-five hundred dollars. I guess we'll have to keep looking. We'll have to find something smaller."

Lynda's face dropped. Franny glanced sideways at John and then back to Jeremiah. "Well, thirty-five hundred dollars is exactly how much I want for it, so if you want it, you've got yourself a deal."

"You must be joking," said Jeremiah.

"Franny never jokes," said John with a chuckle. "If you've got a cheque, you'd better write it real quick before she changes her mind."

Jeremiah wasn't about to look a gift horse in the mouth, so he pulled out his cheque book and wrote the cheque with a flourish. He suspected Franny had taken pity on Lynda and the kids, and he showed his gratitude by thanking her profusely and inviting her to join them at the campground for dinner.

"Well, bless you and thank you very much for asking me. I can't come tonight, but I'm invited to your family dinner tomorrow evening, so I'll see you there. Benny and Phil were old fishing buddies."

John helped Jeremiah hook the trailer onto the hitch, and they all climbed into the van again, this time with big smiles on their faces. Waving goodbye to Franny, they headed back to the campground. When David and the professor saw the van pull in with a trailer that looked brand new behind it, they hurried over to help clear the lot and guide the trailer in.

"Man, what a beauty," said Gordon. "You went all out."

"Lynda's over the moon with joy," said Jeremiah. "You'll never believe the deal we made. Where do I fill up with water, John?"

"The hose is right in the middle of the campground. It's two hundred feet long, so it should extend to your trailer."

He pointed it out to him and helped with the hookup for the lights and sewer. The gas had to be turned on. Jeremiah was a happy man. He couldn't understand why Franny didn't sell the trailer for what it was worth, so he mentioned it to John.

"The trailer reminds her of Benny, and she's tried to sell it for a couple of months now. She didn't want to sell it to people who wouldn't take care of it, so she turned down a couple of offers. Benny was very fussy about his trailer. I think the babies won her over. Don't fret about it. If she didn't want you to have it, you wouldn't have gotten it, no matter how much you offered her. Franny's funny that way."

"Well, I'm grateful, whatever her reason," said Jeremiah.

Holly invited Magen to join them for a swim in the river. Albert pointed out a great swimming hole. It was very deep, and a makeshift diving board had been set up in a large tree. There was a sand bar and rock pile surrounding the swimming hole that protected the swimmers from the rushing pull of the river.

Just as they were ready to leave for the swim, Phil arrived with his wife, Kate, and his eighteen-year-old twin daughters, Lorrie and Peggy. Not only were they twins, but it was impossible to tell which was which—the kids were fascinated by this anomaly. Both girls were tall and beautiful and had sandy coloured hair.

"Don't worry," said Lorrie after introductions were made, "sometimes my mother can't tell us apart." She held up her hand. "I'm Lorrie, and I'm wearing a blue bracelet. I like blue, so I wear it a lot, if that helps."

Peggy held up her hand to display a red beaded bracelet. "I'm Peggy, and I have a red bracelet. My favourite colour is red. I see you're going for a swim. Do you mind if we join you?"

"Please do," said Holly. "I have extra suits if you'd like to borrow them."

"Oh, don't worry," said Lorrie, "we always wear our suits under our clothes. Mom calls us a couple of mermaids because we're in the water every chance we get, and we like to be prepared."

"That's Holly's favourite expression," said Bonnie. "You'd think she was a boy scout."

"Mine too," said Peggy. "I heard you were scuba divers. When would you like to go diving? We know all the best spots, so we'll take you there."

"That's why we're here," said Paul. "The professor told us there were super spots in Crowsnest Lake. He said there were sunken wrecks that we can explore."

"Yeah," said Lorrie, "and there's much more than that. Let's just go for a swim now, and we'll plan what we're going to do after dinner."

"Cool," said Holly. "I can't wait. You can change and leave your clothes in our motorhome or tent, whichever you prefer."

"We'll just leave them in your tent."

The twins were in and out of the tent in less than five minutes. Lorrie was wearing a blue bikini, and Peggy was wearing red. *Figures*, thought Holly. They led the way to the swimming hole and climbed the rope ladder to the diving board. The twins proved they were fearless as they did double back flips off the board into the water.

The swimming hole was as large as a regular sized pool. A small section was fenced off for small children, and there were signs prohibiting children under twelve from swimming without supervision by adults. The river was very wide at this point, and beyond the sandbar and rocks it was very rapid.

Peggy challenged them all to a race. They discovered she was a fast swimmer, but she was a bit deflated when Paul slipped by her with his Australian crawl and made her look like she was doing the dog paddle. The others didn't care. They expected Paul to win. His blue ribbons proved he could swim like the fastest fish in the sea. Peggy came in second, Ted was third, and the other girls stayed pretty much together.

"My sister's not used to coming in second," said Lorrie. "I've never seen anybody swim like Paul. He's amazing."

"I agree," said Holly. "Paul's a certified lifeguard and has won nine championship trophies and a ton of blue ribbons. Top swimmers have challenged him, and he always wins. He says that someday someone will beat him, that there's always somebody better, but so far it hasn't happened."

"Well, maybe the fact that she was beaten by a champion will help to soothe her shocked spirit," Laurie murmured.

A moment later, her jaw dropped in surprise when Peggy walked up to Paul and congratulated him on a super race.

"Thank you," said Paul. "You're pretty fast yourself."

"Wow," said Laurie, "that's a first. But then again, I've never seen anyone beat her before."

"Did you see that?" said Peggy when she'd accepted the outcome and swallowed her pride. "Paul moves like a bullet through the water. I've never seen anything like that before."

"We know," said Ted. "Neither have we. But you did great yourself. You held your own against a champion swimmer who has yet to be beaten and came in second. We'll fill you in later on his many other achievements."

"A champion, eh?"

"That's right."

"Umm ... well, that's okay then."

"Okay," said Holly, "let's go and dry off, and we can plan what we're going to do after supper."

When they arrived back at the motorhome, they discovered two more of the professor's brothers had arrived in motorhomes with their families. The brothers looked so much alike that they appeared like quadruplets. Their burnished red hair was like sunburst halos, and they were each well over six feet three inches in height and built like massive warriors.

"Come and meet my brothers and their families," the professor said invitingly to Holly and the rest of the kids. "You've met Phillip and Kate. Now this is Keith and his wife, Brianna, and their twin girls, Sabrina and Mara, who are fourteen years old. Meet Holly, Paul, Bonnie, and Ted. And this is my brother, Lawrence, his wife, Olivia, and their sons, Manville and Stuart. Believe it or not, they're also twins, eleven years old. Lorrie and Peggy are Phillip and Kate's twin girls. It's almost like a twins' convention. Now I think everybody's been introduced."

When the greetings and salutations were over, Susan, Kate, and Heather invited everyone to sit around the picnic tables that had been set and decorated with pretty tablecloths and flowered centrepieces. Phil and Kate had hired a caterer for their first family reunion meal together, who rolled several carts of food into the campground. For once, Susan and Heather could sit and be waited on. There were twenty-nine people around the tables, and places were set for four more.

"I hope Dennis and Lara aren't having trouble on the road," said Phillip. "They should have arrived by now."

"Are you sure they're coming?" Lawrence asked. "Last I heard, Dennis couldn't get time off."

"Yes, well he said they might be late because he had to work a half day. He couldn't find anyone to take the half day shift."

"What does he work at?" David asked.

"He's an EMT in Calgary," said Phil. "Don't worry. He'll be here."

"Well, at least he doesn't have to come too far," said David.

The caterers set the steaming hot food on the table. It was quite a banquet. Just as everyone began to serve themselves, a motorhome pulled in. The driver was honking the horn to announce his arrival.

"Well, it's about time," Phil shouted as he bounded up from the table to welcome the latecomers.

Another mirror image of the professor climbed down from the vehicle and threw his arms around Phil and Kate. He was followed by his family—his wife, Lara, and his seventeen-year-old children, Sally and Charlie.

"Did they clone everybody in your family?" Heather asked Gordon jokingly. She was in awe. "It's like you were all produced by a Xerox machine. They all have red hair, and they all look alike."

"Really, Heather, the only ones you can't tell apart are Lorrie and Peggy. Even their folks sometimes can't tell which is which, and their hair is sandy red."

"True, but it's very confusing," Heather observed. "I'm very good at remembering people, but they're usually all quite different. This is like *Alice in Wonderland*. I think I've fallen down the rabbit hole. It's mystifying, but rather wonderful. Do you feel like you're talking to yourself when you talk to your brothers?"

He laughed uproariously. "I never thought of it like that, but now that you mention it, that might have something to do with the reason we haven't socialized or kept in touch. I'm kidding," he said when he saw the look on her face. "We just seem to have gotten so caught up in our jobs and lives that we've left family and close friends behind.

"I was actually a loner by choice until I met Holly and her friends and family. It was just Socrates and me … a situation of my own making. I can only blame myself. But since I met you, my life has taken on new meaning. I actually like being around other people now. Another psychologist might find that very interesting, since I am a psychologist myself … the stuff books are written about."

"Well, I hope now that you've changed your outlook on life you'll include your family. The fact that you haven't seen them in ten years is rather shameful. They seem to be a lovely family, and if I'm going to be part of it, Gordon, then I'm going to insist on a reunion every year, or have some of them visit for Christmas, especially those who live in B.C."

"I'd go for that. I have missed them, and I do keep in touch now and then by email. When the five of us played high school or college football, we confused all the players. Each time a player on the other team got the ball, he thought he was being tackled by the same guy no matter which way he turned. The spectators got a great kick out of it, though the refs could never tell who had the ball."

Heather roared with that great raucous belly laugh of hers.

"What's so funny?" he asked.

"You are." She was still giggling. "I can just see it now. Five huge redheads, with hair like the burning bush, charging up the field like Irish warriors, and the surprised looks on the faces of the other team as they floundered to get out of your way. You should have been wearing kilts. It must have been a sight to behold." She laughed so hard she was choking.

He laughed along with her at the thought.

Holly and her friends engaged Sally and Charlie with their plans for the evening. They too were redheads. Sally's hair was a halo of curls, and Charlie's was gelled and stood up like spikes. To everyone's surprise, they were also scuba divers, although their experience was limited.

"We just took the course last month," said Charlie. "A school friend of ours drowned in June. She wasn't a very good swimmer, and she got caught in a current that pulled her down. We decided to learn drown-proofing methods, and my other friend suggested we learn to scuba dive. We brought our equipment with us because Dad said there were lots of places to scuba dive in the Pass."

"We'll feel much safer diving with you since you've had so much experience," said Sally.

"There are seven experienced divers here, nine if you count Daddy and the professor," said Holly. "You'll be fine, as long as you follow the rules."

For camping fare, the meal was outstanding. The baron of beef was so tender that the knife sliced through it like it was butter. It was complemented with a broccoli and cheese casserole and stuffed potatoes topped with all the trimmings. Asparagus tips and carrots rounded out the menu. A peach cobbler for dessert topped off the evening's meal.

"We've never had food like this when we've gone camping," said Lara.

"We don't even eat like this when we're not camping," added Kim.

"Well," said Phil, "Kate and I figured we should kill the fatted calf to welcome all the family to our reunion. We've been apart too long. There are still two people missing. We're hoping they'll get here tonight."

"Who's missing, Dad?" Peggy asked.

"Your Aunt Molly and Uncle Robert. I hope they get here tonight. It's quite a drive from Winnipeg."

Holly asked Peggy if there was a dive shop in Blairmore. They each had two tanks of air, which would only last for two dives.

"Yes, there's a dive shop on Third Avenue. They have everything we'll need."

"That's good," said Holly. "Where do you suggest we go after dinner? And is it close?"

"You passed it on the way here," Peggy said. "Crowsnest Lake has sunken wrecks and a cave with ancient aboriginal artwork on the walls."

"Oh, this is going to be fantastic," Sally enthused. "We haven't had the chance to explore anything like that. Do we have to get permission to enter the cave?"

"No, you just can't go alone," said Lorrie. "It's for your own safety, and you should also let someone responsible know where you're going just in case you have a problem or an accident. Otherwise, no one would ever find you, and you could be lost forever."

"If you're trying to frighten us, you're doing a good job of it," said Charlie. "Don't worry, we'll stick like glue to the rest of you. We're still feeling our way, and we're not ready to head out on our own. As twins, Sally and I do most things together, mainly because we enjoy each other's company. A lot of siblings don't, but I think that's because of a difference in age. Since we were born together, we pretty much stick together."

"I can understand that," said Holly. "Paul, Bonnie, and I have been close friends since we were about three years old, and we do everything together. In fact, we're closer than friends … we're almost like triplets. Ted joined us this summer, and we're so happy he did. He rounded out the foursome very nicely. It's a gift to have someone close to you that you can depend on no matter what."

"Holly's the one who makes all the plans," said Paul. "She has the imagination to dream up new adventures for us, and we just go along with them. She's kept us busy all summer."

"Let's thank Uncle Phil and Aunt Kate for this beautiful meal and head out to the lake. By the time we get there and hike to the spot where we want to dive, it will be time to enter the water," said Holly. "You can all ride on the backs of our motorbikes, but you'll have to wear your equipment … at least what we haven't got room for on the bikes."

"That's okay," said Peggy. "We'll take my car. I have plenty of room for the equipment."

"Super," said Bonnie. "Where's your car parked?"

"Over in the car park. Just follow us on your bikes."

"Right behind you," said Paul.

Crowsnest Lake

THE KIDS PULLED DOWN ONTO THE EASTERN SHORELINE OF CROWSNEST LAKE and lined up their vehicles. There were two trailers and one tent already there, and a couple of young teenage boys were playing cards at a picnic table beside one of the trailers. There was a derelict building that Peggy said used to be a dance hall, and the ruins of an old building that looked like some sort of factory on the right.

A couple of ramshackle shacks were visible through the trees along the left bank, and a shed that looked like an outhouse was hidden in the bushes. The kids stood transfixed as they gazed out over the water. A whistle sounded and a train chugged slowly round the bend as it followed the curve along the edge of the lake. They waved at the engineer, and he waved back.

A fisherman was standing on the bank with his line in the water, patiently waiting for a rainbow trout to bite. An aluminum boat was out in the middle of the lake. There were two men in it trolling slowly for rainbow with a small motor, and they appeared so peaceful. The purple mountain backdrop that encircled the lake was absolutely breathtaking.

"Wow! This is beautiful," said Holly, and the others agreed with her. "We could set our tents up here if you like. Is there a charge to camp?" she asked Peggy.

"No. You're just expected to clean up after yourself and take your garbage away with you. It's a great spot to camp. The cave is over there to the right just above the railway tracks, and the submerged railway car wreck is in that area at seventy or eighty feet. There's also a sunken barge, but I'm not quite sure just where it went down. This all happened around 1929. You'd think there'd be a plaque or a commemorative plate to mark the spot, but there isn't."

"I wonder if anyone in town knows the history of the occasion," said Ted.

"I imagine we could find it if we googled the Internet," said Holly.

"You might be right. Let's do that tonight," suggested Paul.

They hiked along the railway tracks till they came to the cave. Within a few minutes, they were ready to enter the water. They climbed gingerly down the rocks, being careful not to turn an ankle on the sliding shale, and slipped into the water to discover it was freezing cold. A continuous flow of ice cold water gushed like a waterfall out of the rocks above, and it took a while for the suits to warm up. *We should have worn our Farmer Johns and Farmer Janes along with our Artic hoods*, thought Holly.

Charlie and Sally had been instructed to stay with Ted and not to lose sight of him. Paul said he would also keep an eye on them. As locals, Peggy and Lorrie led the way. The others stayed close, making sure they didn't lose sight of their buddies. Ted and Paul were worried about the rookie twins, since they hadn't been below the sixty-foot level, but the siblings followed the rules and stayed with their leaders.

Like Slocan Lake, this lake had areas that hadn't been measured for depth. Many locals believed it was bottomless in those areas, so there could very well be sunken wrecks that would never be found. Crowsnest Lake was also known for its terrifying storms.

Peggy and Lorrie knew where they were going, so the group followed them. Holly and her team noticed the difference between the lake flora and that of the coastal waters and were enchanted by the beautiful colours. The setting sun cast a sparkling silver gleam over a school of rainbow trout as they swam by, and Charlie and Sally pointed excitedly to them. Suddenly, out of nowhere, a lone scuba diver appeared. He was as startled by the group as they were of him, and he stared for a minute before doing a one eighty and swimming quickly for the far shore.

Hmm … I wonder where his buddy is, Holly thought. She suddenly saw a humungous shape below and signalled the others, but they'd seen it too. Ted and Paul signalled that they would go down and check the wreck out first and would signal if it was safe for them to follow. The others waited patiently, treading water, while Ted and Paul dropped down about twenty feet to scout the area. The guys were looking for danger areas where they might get entangled in nets or broken flotsam, or holes they might fall through and become trapped. The wreck was definitely a railway car lying on its side.

They were at seventy feet, but where was the other one? They'd been told there were two. Plants were growing through the doors and windows, and fish were swimming in and out like they were playing a game. Barnacles and marine life parasites clung possessively to the hulk. Ted signalled that they should ascend, so they kicked for the surface to join the others waiting patiently for the signal to descend.

The kids could hardly contain their excitement, but as they swam inside the hulk and saw the iron bases of the seats bolted to the floor, their imaginations began to run away on them, taking them back to the dreadful moments of the accident. Imagining the people made them feel queasy. *Were there children?* They were confronted with the distressing picture of the travellers, who felt so blissfully safe in the hands of the railroad company. Then they felt the passengers' sheer terror and disorientation as the train left the track and sank into the water. They internalized the shock and horror of the victims when they realized they were drowning.

Were their bodies recovered, or are they buried here in eternal sleep in this icy cold water? Did all the passengers—men, women, and children—die because of equipment failure? Was there a rock slide, or did the engineer fall asleep? They must research what kind of accident caused this. *Were any of the passengers saved?*

Holly felt claustrophobic and gave the signal that she wanted to surface, so they ascended slowly to the top. It was a pretty solemn group of young people that swam for the bank. They climbed out and sat on the rocks, staring quietly at the water for a few moments.

"I don't know why I feel so shaken up," Holly said. "I've seen wrecks before, but these were people who didn't have a thought that they might be in peril. An accident on land, maybe, but not a thought of an accident in water riding on a train. We must find out what happened. It won't make any difference now, but I'd like to know."

"I agree," said Paul. "Maybe there was a rock slide, and even though the train slows down to come around this bend, the engineer might not have noticed it in time to stop the train. You can't stop a train like you can a car. Or maybe the track was deliberately destroyed by criminals in order to rob the train's passengers. Instead of causing it to stop, the train was derailed, causing mass murder."

"You're so right," said Bonnie. "We have to ask questions when we go back to town."

"Who do you think we should ask?" Holly asked Laurie.

"Well, if my dad doesn't know, he'll know who to ask. I just knew the train wreck was here, but I don't know the history. It was way before our time … before my dad's time too. Tourists seem to have more interest in it than locals. Now that we're scuba diving, we've started to take an interest in the caves and lake wrecks."

"I want to come back and explore the wreck, but I'd like to know some of the history before we do," said Holly. "We'll bring our tents here tomorrow. But before we go, I'd like to have a look at the cave."

"Sure," said Peggy. "It's hard to reach, because it's very close to the tracks and almost a straight climb just above them. You'll need good lighting."

"We have headlamps with us and underwater flashlights," said Holly. "If we need anything more than that, we have lamps that throw light about twenty feet in the blackest cave. But they're packed in the motorhome. We can bring those with us tomorrow."

"Cool," said Peggy. "We'll need those when we go farther in, but the headlamps will give us a pretty good idea what the cave has to offer. I have to warn you … there might be dangerous crevices and maybe crevasses, so you'll need the other lamps if you plan to go in more than fifteen feet, and we should all be attached to a rope for safety."

"Have you been in the cave?" Ted asked her.

"Just a few feet," Peggy said, "but I've talked to kids who say they've gone farther in. They say it's pretty scary, and there are channels that you could get lost in. There's about four feet of water just inside the entrance. I don't know if the water recedes farther in. The kids who say they've gone in brag a lot, but I don't think they have the big lanterns."

"We'll bring what we have with us tomorrow," said Paul. "We'd better bring our Farmer Johns and Farmer Janes with us tomorrow. This lake is colder than the ocean. Those poor people who drowned on the train would have died almost immediately from hypothermia, even if they could swim."

The kids agreed. They slipped back into the water and swam below the surface till they reached the entrance to the cave. Then they climbed up the rock-strewn bank and over the tracks and decided to leave their air tanks at the entrance. They wouldn't need them in four feet of water, but they would need their headlamps, because the cave was pitch black.

Magen and the twins hadn't brought theirs with them, but they made a mental note to pack them tomorrow. Peggy and Laurie decided they would bring a tent as well, and Magen could share their tent. Holly and Bonnie would share with Sally, and Charlie would bunk with Paul and Ted. It would be pretty snug with three in a tent, but they would manage. They all had sleeping bags, and Holly would bring her famous cooler duffle bag. There were lots of left-overs from the trip.

"I think we should check out the camp at the other end of the lake," said Holly. "Maybe they have facilities that would make it more convenient for us."

"Yes, they do have cabins and washrooms, and I think there is a little convenience store," said Laurie. "We've never stayed there, since we live so close to the lake, but it might be fun. If the weather turned bad, we could move into a cabin."

"I think they also have boats for hire," said Peggy. "We've seen boats at the pier when we've been scuba diving, and there are rafts and diving boards. Sometimes they have windsurfing races when the wind is high. You'd have to wear your scuba diving gear for that, because if you think it was cold in the water, I've seen people turn blue and almost freeze to death windsurfing in a bikini."

"Okay then, I nominate Ted and Paul as the leaders," said Holly. "Ted is a professional tracker and has more experience in caves than the rest of us. Is everybody okay with that?" They all agreed. "They will scout out a few feet ahead of the rest of us, and if they say stop, you must all agree to stop. This is important. If you have a problem with that, then you shouldn't go in."

Since they all agreed, Ted took command.

"Okay, guys, let's get going," he said. "If you have a headlamp or flashlight, turn them on. We'll be better equipped tomorrow, so we won't be going more than a few feet into the cave today. The roof of the tunnel is very low, and the water at the entrance is probably caused by all the water that's flowing out of the mountain and down over the entrance, or it could be a spring. Hopefully, it will be drier inside as we proceed. We don't know what we're going to find, so be very careful."

Ted tied a thin nylon rope around his body and told everybody to take hold of the rope, wrap it around their wrists, and not let go. He swam into the blackness of the cave, and the others followed. Paul switched on his powerful flashlight and shone it into the darkness beyond to light the way, but no sooner did the group cautiously swim towards the black hole than a frightful squealing and rustling emitted from the blackness of the cave. The girls all began to scream and were bumping into each other as they turned in the water and stroked frantically towards the exit of the cave. Suddenly, a colony of bats swooshed over their heads and zoomed for the exit. The girls were hysterical with fear. Some even swallowed water and began to choke.

"Just stay low and cover your heads," Paul shouted.

"They won't hurt you," said Ted. "They're more afraid of you than you are of them."

"Don't you believe it," said Bonnie. "I'm shaking like a leaf."

"No wonder the locals don't want to explore this cave," Laurie whimpered.

The girls were all whimpering and had their arms wrapped around their heads. Holly, once she got over her fright, tried to calm them down.

"Well, at least they weren't wolves," Bonnie said. She'd never forgotten the night they spent in a cave on Garibaldi Mountain while a wolf pack howled and threatened to commandeer the cave. That was one scary night; however, a colony of bats was just as frightening.

"The bats have gone," said Ted. "They won't come back as long as we're in here. We scared them off. I suppose Paul and I should have checked the interior out before you all entered the cave. That was our fault. We'll be sure to check it out tomorrow before we start to explore. I have to admit, it was a bit of a rush when they all flew over our heads. It took a minute to figure out what was coming at us."

Charlie was trying to sound macho by laughing, but his laugh was rather high pitched for a seventeen-year-old, and he sounded like a nervous girl. Sally kicked him in the shin.

"Stop it," she shouted. "You're behaving like an idiot."

"Ouch! Ouch! Ouch!" Now he was whimpering like the girls and frantically rubbing his leg. "Why did you kick me, Sally? That hurt!"

"Okay, I'm sorry, but you shouldn't be laughing when somebody's scared," she scolded him. "Those bats frightened me half to death, and you too, if you'd just admit it."

"Yeah, you're right," he reluctantly agreed. "I suppose you want to leave now?"

"I'm over my fright now," she said. "Though like Bonnie said, I'm still shaking a bit. But I'll go along with what everybody else decides. If we're going to be exploring caves and wrecks, I suppose I'd better get used to unexpected and scary surprises."

"I think we'd better give it up for today," said Holly. "It's getting late, and we should be getting back to town. We'll come back in the morning, after breakfast, but before we set up. I think we should take a look at the camp at the other end of the lake and decide if we want to stay there or come back to this end. We're having a marshmallow roast and family singsong tonight down by the river, and we'll tell some stories around the fire. It's a good way to get to know all the cousins."

"You're right," said Paul. "It's 9:05 p.m. I can't believe the time went by so fast. We'll check in with the camp in the morning and see what they have to offer."

They decided to swim back to the east shore rather than hiking. Walking would mean being loaded down with all their heavy scuba gear.

When they were in the water, the scuba gear didn't feel heavy at all. They slipped into the water and headed for the eastern shore. They noticed the water was warmer in the shallow end. Soon they were on their way back to town full of plans for the rest of the week.

When they pulled into the campground, they were met with shouts of welcome. The family were all there with chairs and benches pulled together in a circle around a humongous campfire. Everybody had a stick, and they were all busy toasting marshmallows, which they added to some very tasty crackers to make smores. Willie ran to meet them, clutching two sticks that were already peeled and pared to a nice point.

"These are for Ted and Paul," he said. "Ted's going to teach me to swim. Dad too!"

"I did promise that, didn't I," said Ted. "Well, we'll try to work a lesson in tomorrow. Let's see how our plans work out."

Ted asked Sam for his cell phone number and promised to get back to him after they'd explored the cave and taken another look at the railway car.

"Just have your swimming trunks ready, and I'll call you when we're ready to go. We'll be setting up our camp tomorrow morning at the lake," he said, "but I'll have some time in the afternoon after we've finished exploring, and you and Willie can take a lesson together. I guarantee I won't let you drown."

"Well, if it hadn't been for you guys, Willie and I would both have drowned. Do you think it might be too late for me to learn? I've always been a little bit afraid of the water."

"You're never too old to learn, and don't forget that we'll have Paul, a champion swimmer and certified lifeguard. Once you learn to swim, you'll never be afraid of the water again, and you'll never need to be saved from drowning again."

Sam had brightened up. "We'll be ready when you call. I need to do this for Willie so he won't be afraid in the water like I am … and for me too, I guess."

John had joined the group around the fire, and he was regaling them with stories about the Pass from days of long ago. He told them about Dan Mulligan, the old prospector who struck it rich prowling the hills around the Lost Lemon Mine, and of how many had lost their lives prowling the same hills looking for their piece of the rainbow. "They say old Dan's spirit still walks the hills with his mule and dog, Benji. Different people have said they've seen him."

"Super cool," said Holly. The kids' eyes were wide as saucers. "Do you know the story of the railway cars that sunk into the lake, and what happened to the passengers?"

"Yes. Well, that was a long time ago," John said. "I believe it was 1929 or thereabouts. There are several stories about that. We didn't have computers in those days, and word of mouth is not always accurate. Some say the engineer fell asleep. How could they tell, since nobody lived to tell about it? Others say it was rocks on the line, and there were many other stories of various suppositions. All I know is that the passengers were a mix of men, women, and children, and they all died when the train left the tracks and deep sixed into the ice-cold waters of Crowsnest Lake. They never found any of them, as far as I know. That lake is a graveyard. I don't know how you kids can swim in it."

Holly was as mesmerized and transfixed as the others. "Do you know where we could find the history about that and other historical events in the Pass?" she inquired.

"You could try the Interpretative Centre. It's just up the road a few miles at the town of Frank, or what's left of it."

"What do you mean by what's left of it?" Holly asked. "Did something happen to the town?"

"Something did indeed happen," said John. "Three quarters of the town was buried about a hundred years ago. That's another occasion when most everybody died. Well, not exactly. There was only one life saved in the south end of town … a tiny little baby. Can you believe it? Most of the town was wiped out in about five minutes, and only one little baby survived in the south end. A few houses, including the bank and a couple of businesses at the north edge of the town, escaped the devastation, and a few people survived."

"What do you mean?" Holly's face revealed the shock she felt. Everyone was hunched over to catch every word. "Did a bomb drop? What happened?"

"The whole east side of Turtle Mountain fell down! It wiped out everything and everyone in the town of Frank while they slept, except for the few people at the north end," said John. "A man, one of the survivors, climbed over the fallen rock and ran over a mile to stop an oncoming train, the Spokane Flyer. It was packed with sleeping passengers. The engineer was unaware of the devastation up ahead, and if he hadn't been warned, there would have been another tragedy."[1]

"Dear God," said Susan as she clasped the sides of her face.

"Who found the little baby?" Bonnie whispered.

"I don't know, but they could tell you at the Interpretive Centre. They not only have the whole history, but they know the name of the baby. It was a little girl, and she lived well into her nineties. You can stand in the Interpretive Centre on an overhanging deck and take pictures of the destruction. You can't believe it till you see it."

"We will definitely have to go and see that," said Ted.

"Yeah," said John. "The Blackfoot natives call it the 'Mountain That Moves or Walks,' and they warned people before it happened that it was going to come down on the town of Frank, but nobody listened. They also warned that it is going to come down again, but on the north side next time, and again, nobody is listening. People are still living there."[2]

"The mountain that moves," Heather mused. "How could the natives know that?"

"The natives know more about the earth signs and what the mountain is saying when it rumbles than some of the geologists, and I would move if I lived there. I wouldn't take a chance with my family," said John.

"Do you know anything about the mines in the Pass?" Ted asked.

"Well, I know there were a lot of lives lost in the mines. Hillcrest Collieries owned the mine in Hillcrest. In 1914, the worst mine disaster in Canadian history was caused by an explosion. It was the third worst mine disaster in the world at that time. They lost 189 men, more than half their work force. There have been other explosions in mines around the Pass, but nothing as bad as that one."[*]

---

[1] The events surrounding the Frank Slide actually happened in 1903.

[2] This is an historical account.

"Are any of the mines still working?" Paul asked.

"No, they were shut down years ago," said John. "Too many accidents, and too many deaths."

"Are there any tours through the mines?" Holly asked.

"Not now," said John. "Not since the young couple disappeared about twenty years ago. They'd been warned not to go into the mines without a guide, but it's believed they were nosing around in some of the mines in the Pass, and then it was reported that they'd disappeared. They were never heard of again." [3*]

"How awful," said Heather. "Did they send out a search party?"

"Oh yes," said John. "Hundreds of people searched for them, but they were unsuccessful. Then people began searching the hills for the Lost Lemon Mine, thinking the young couple may have heard the legend and decided to try their luck."

"The Lost Lemon Mine?" said Holly. "What were they looking for?"

"Gold!" Now John really had their attention.

"Gold?" exclaimed Holly. "Is there gold here?"

"Well, you couldn't prove it by me, but old Dan Mulligan said there was, and he certainly struck it rich somewhere. But he kept his secret and took it to the grave."

"Is there a legend about the location of the mine?" Paul asked.

"Just that the sun shines through a hole in the rock at noon at the top of the mountain and points to the spot where the mother lode lies."

"Which mountain?" Charlie asked. He was twitching with excitement. "Let's go and try to find it."

"Lots of luck, kid," said John. "Hundreds of men have tried to find it in the last hundred years without success. Old Dan Mulligan didn't pass the location on to anyone."

The professor began to play "The Blue Canadian Rockies" on his mouth organ, and one by one the campers began to sing. Holly and the other kids ran to the motorhome to get their instruments, and Bonnie pulled hers out of her saddlebag. In five minutes, they were tuned up and ready to go. Peggy and Laurie ran home to get their guitars and grabbed their dad's banjo too. When they arrived back at the campground, Peggy

---

[3*] An historical event.

handed the banjo to her father and then joined in with the band like they'd been playing together for years. They sounded like they were straight from Nashville.

"Is that Dad's old banjo?" Gordon asked Phillip.

"Yes. What do you think?" Phil handed the banjo to his brother.

"Wow! What did you do to it?" asked Gordon. "The mother of pearl frets look new, and the mother of pearl casing with the gilt trim is beautiful."

"Well, it was pretty beaten up," Phil said, "but the sound was still great, so I had it restored.

"They did a great job." Gordon was really impressed. "It looks brand new. Well, let's hear you play it, brother."

Phillip grinned and stepped over to the makeshift band. Without losing a beat, he jumped right into the "Irish Washerwoman" along with the other musicians. Sally found a level spot and did a lively Irish jig while the campers clapped along. Other campers drifted over to join in the fun, and whatever song anyone requested, the band swung right into it. They played all the old campfire songs, and when some people asked for a familiar hymn, like "Amazing Grace" or "How Great Thou Art," the band immediately played it while the campers sang along.

Susan made the request for Ted to sing a solo. The band discussed it for a moment and then he decided to sing "Island in the Sun." David also joined in with his steel guitar, and Gordon beat out the rumba rhythm on Ted's bongo drum. Those who hadn't heard the group before were amazed at Ted's beautiful classical voice, which had them thinking of island beaches and palm trees. The girls harmonized in the chorus.

The audience whistled and applauded when he finished, and they shouted for more.

"Does anyone have a special request?" Ted asked.

An old man at the back of the crowd raised his hand.

"Yes, sir," Ted asked. "What would you like to hear?"

"Do you happen to know 'Country Roads'?" he asked.

"Yes, sir. 'Country Roads' it is."

The band played an intro, and Ted began to sing. The girls harmonized again in the chorus. Ted was able to change his voice to suit the genre of music. Now he sounded like a western cowboy. His many years on stage in his mother's musicals had taught him to fit into any type of music. By the time they were into the second chorus, all the campers had joined in.

Night had fallen and the fire burned low as the campers started to drift away. Holly suggested they should play "Irene Goodnight" and call it a night. If they wanted to get away to the lake early in the morning, they needed to get a good night's sleep. When the song was over, they tidied up the campsite and threw water and sand on the fire. Susan handed them each a hot chocolate, and they sipped it slowly.

Peggy and Laurie promised to meet them at 8:30 the following morning. They would pack all their scuba equipment and the tents in the trunk of Peggy's car, and Sally and Charlie could ride with them. Magen would ride on the back of Holly's bike. Willie wanted to go with them, but Ted promised he would see him in the afternoon. When they'd finalized their plans, they said goodnight to their parents and the cousins.

Holly and Bonnie were happy to find that their tent was completely dry and aired out. They could have stayed in the motorhome, but they preferred to sleep in the great outdoors as long as they weren't in a storm like they were at Slocan Lake.

"This was a great day," said Holly. "In spite of the bats."

"I don't know," said Bonnie. "Little mice with wings flying at my hair is not my idea of a great anything, but at least it wasn't a pack of wolves. I suppose it could have been worse."

"Yeah," Holly agreed. "It could have been a bear."

"You're not making me feel any better," said Bonnie.

"Sorry! We won't go into the cave tomorrow till Ted and Paul check it out. They don't seem to be afraid of anything." Holly pulled her green fleece pyjamas out of her backpack. They were so comfy cozy, and she loved them. "I'm wearing my warm fleecy pyjamas," she said, "because it gets really cold in the mountains at night."

"Me too," said Bonnie, "but I just hope nobody yells 'Fire,' or they'll think the Easter bunny has been turned loose if they see me in these."

Holly laughed uproariously when she saw the huge floppy feet on Bonnie's pyjamas. "Yeah, the two of us are a rare sight. I look like Santa's elf. We'd better not let anybody see us wandering around the camp like this, or they'll be getting the butterfly nets out for us."

Both girls got into a fit of the giggles as they snuggled down into their Artic sleeping bags and pulled the hoods over their heads. They were still giggling after Holly turned out the lantern. The sounds of the rapids rushing fiercely over the rocks, in concert with the soft breezes spreading the fragrance of wisteria like fairy dust over the undulating leaves in the trees, soon lulled the girls to sleep.

Thieves in the Pass

CHAPTER 4

THE TRUNK OF PEGGY'S CAR WAS PACKED WITH SCUBA GEAR AND TENTS. Charlie's and Sally's gear was included. At the last minute, Holly threw her accordion in, and the others ran off to get their instruments. Magen would ride with Holly, but she'd also packed her scuba gear into the trunk of the car.

The saddlebags and motorbike trunks were packed full for the short journey to Crowsnest Lake. They'd finished their breakfast, and Holly was cramming food from the motorhome's fridge into her duffle bag. Thankfully, there were plenty of leftovers from the previous evening's dinner, and Susan said she was going grocery shopping for fresh food in the afternoon and insisted Holly help herself.

Susan never wanted the kids to go hungry, so she was only too happy to let Holly clean the fridge out. Since her mother loved cooking and baking, there was always a terrific display of food, and when she opened the duffle bag, Holly always got the credit for it. But when the diners thanked her for the food, she always said, "You can thank my mom. She's the cook."

Ted asked Sam for his cell number and promised to call him when he was free to give him and Willie a swimming lesson. "It would probably be in the afternoon," he told him. Sam was happy about that, as he would be joining the other adults the next day on the golf course.

By 8:45 a.m., they were on their way. Magen was thrilled to ride on the rumble seat of Holly's bike. She'd never been on a motorbike before. Holly's team followed Peggy's car, and a few minutes after nine o'clock, they were pulling into the camp at Crowsnest Lake.

The campsite was equipped with cabins, a large hall, and other buildings; it was laid out neatly in sections for tenting and trailers or mobile homes. A man approached them, and Holly and her team stepped off their bikes to greet him. They pulled off their helmets, and Paul offered his hand in greeting.

"Hello," said Paul. "We'd like to know if we can camp here."

"I'm Andy, the caretaker here. Where are you from?" the man inquired.

"We're from the West Coast ... Vancouver and Lions Bay area. My name is Paul Castles," he said. "We're visiting friends in Blairmore. Some of our group are staying at the campground there."

"Why aren't you staying there?" asked Andy with a not-too-friendly look.

"We're scuba divers, and we like to be close to the water," Ted broke in. "Hi, I'm Ted Lumley. Do you have camping space for us? We have tents."

Andy noticed Peggy and Laurie in the car. He approached the driver's side. "I've seen you here and in town. You aren't from the coast," he said in an unwelcoming voice.

"No, we live in the Pass. We're Peggy and Laurie Clayborn. You know our dad, Phil Clayborn."

"That's right. Why do you want to stay here when you live so close? We don't rent to people who want to party. We don't allow drinking parties. We have children here who are vacationing with their parents."

"We don't drink," Holly said. "Is there some reason you don't want us to camp here?"

"We have a situation here," he said. "This morning we woke up to find the camp had been robbed."

"Robbed!" the kids all exclaimed at once. "What was taken, and was anybody hurt?" Holly asked.

"Nobody was hurt. Everybody was sleeping, but when we got up this morning, we discovered that three bicycles, two canoes with their 4 HP motors, and four generators from outside the campers' motor homes and trailers were missing. Nobody heard anything, so the thieves got clean away."

"I wondered why you were asking so many questions," said Ted. "Now I understand. Did you report it to the police?"

"Yes, I just finished talking to them as you drove in. I'm sorry for asking so many questions, but I was just being cautious," explained Andy. "And to add to that, the kids were supposed to have swimming lessons at ten o'clock, and the swimming instructor didn't show up. She was supposed to be coming in from Clairsholm last night, and she phoned yesterday at four o'clock to say she was on the way, but she didn't arrive. I tried to get her on her cell, but there was no answer. I think something must have happened to her. I informed the police that she was missing."

"Don't you think the lake's a bit cold for the kids to be taking swimming lessons?" Holly asked.

"Oh, it's not cold at the edge," Andy said. "It's only when you get into the deeper water that it's cold. It doesn't seem to bother the kids. It's going to be a hot day. They'll be really disappointed that the instructor didn't show up."

Holly and her friends looked at each other with raised eyebrows.

"What do you say, guys?" said Paul. They all nodded their heads "yes."

"Well, this is your lucky day," said Paul. "The kids don't have to be disappointed. We'll teach them to swim."

"Oh, we can't have just anybody who comes in here working with the kids," said Andy. "It has to be a certified swimming instructor."

"Well," said Holly, "you've had a bad day so far, so let's try to make it a little brighter for you. We're all certified scuba divers, and Paul is a certified life guard and champion swimmer, and we would consider it a privilege to teach a swimming class this morning. No charge." They all pulled out their wallets and showed him their certificates of registration.

Andy's face brightened up. "I'll put a call in to Phil Clayborn, just to make sure you're all on the up and up."

"There's just one thing," said Ted. "I promised a twelve-year-old boy and his father that I'd teach them how to swim. Is it okay if they join the class?"

"Absolutely," said Andy. "And for doing this, you can camp here and use all the facilities for free."

"Cool!" they exclaimed in chorus.

Ted plugged Sam's cell number into his phone, and Sam answered immediately. "Hi, Sam! It's Ted here. We're at the lake, and we're going to teach a swimming class at 10:00 a.m. Would you and Willie like to join us? Willie will have fun learning with the other kids."

"Sure thing," said Sam. "We'll leave right away."

Ted gave Sam directions to the camp and asked Andy how many kids would be taking the class. After being told there would be nineteen, he joined the other guys for a discussion.

"This will work out fine," he told the others. "There are nineteen kids for the class. With Sam and Willie, that will make twenty-one. There are nine of us, and since Charlie and Sally are new divers, we'll use them as floaters. They can help anybody who's having a problem, and we can take care of three kids each. Does everybody agree?"

"That sounds great," said Holly. The others nodded in agreement.

As they were conferring, kids of all ages poured out of the RVs and cabins. They were already in their swimwear and excited that they were going to be learning to swim. The kids didn't know that the swim coach was missing. Just then, the RCMP cruiser rolled in, and two officers got out. Andy went to meet them, and some of the camp staff exited the hall. Some curious adult campers gathered around to find out what was being said.

"Hi, Andy," an officer said as he shook the caretaker's hand. "I hear you've had a bit of trouble."

"That's right, Cliff," Andy nodded as he shook the other officer's hand. "Hi, Roland. Nice to see you back again. Thanks for coming so quickly. We've had some items stolen in the middle of the night. The robbers took things that could easily be carried down the lane to a truck. It must have been a truck, because two of the items were canoes."

"What else did they take?" Officer Cliff asked.

"Well, besides the canoes, the paddles, and two 4 HP motors that belonged to the canoes, there were four generators belonging to the campers, trailers, motorhomes, and three bicycles—two boys' and one girls'. There might be other stuff missing; the campers are checking through their things now. They even took towels off the lines. Can you believe it? Nobody heard a thing."

"Can you identify the items that were stolen?" Cliff asked.

"I have receipts and pictures of the canoes and the motors. I don't know what the campers might have to help identify their items."

"Receipts and pictures are good. The receipts will have a model number on them and maybe more," said Officer Roland. "We'll talk to the campers and see what they can come up with. There's been a rash of robberies this past month, all items that can be carried away. We've contacted venues where they could sell these things easily, such as pawn shops and second hand vendors, and we've asked them to look out for items that could be identified. If we find those, we'll probably find the rest. Meanwhile, I would suggest you contact your insurance companies, and don't leave anything valuable out in the open at night."

With that, the officers began their investigation by speaking to all the campers. A truck pulled in and Andy approached it warily, but it was just Sam and a very excited Willie.

"We're full, sir," said Andy. "We have no more space. You'll have to go in to the camp in Blairmore."

"Oh, but we're here for the swimming class," said Sam. "We're looking for Ted Lumley. He's going to teach us to swim."

"Yeah! He said he would teach me to swim like him and Paul," said Willie. "Paul's a champion swimmer, you know!"

"Oh, right," said Andy. "Ted told me you'd be here, and he said Paul was a champion swimmer. We're very lucky they showed up today, because our swim coach is missing."

"They saved me and my dad from drowning," said Willie.

"Yeah," said Sam. "We'd be dead for sure if they hadn't saved us at Slocan Lake. I was about twelve feet under and drowning, and Paul dove down and pulled me up. That's why Willie and I are taking lessons."

"Is that so?" said Andy. "Then the kids are in good hands. God is good. Just follow me; they're over here planning the class."

Willie ran ahead to find Paul and Ted. "Hi, Paul. Hi, Ted," he shouted. "We're ready to swim."

"That's great, Willie," said Ted. "Hi, Sam. Glad you made it. We'll be starting in a few minutes, just as soon as we get all the kids organized. I'll be your teacher, as I promised." He waved all the kids over. "Gather around, kids, and we'll talk about rules."

The kids eagerly made a circle. "Now, you must listen very carefully. There'll be three kids to each teacher, and you must do exactly what the teacher says. It's important that you listen to every word. This is not a game, and knowing the rules can save your life. We're going to teach you how to be safe in the water, no matter how deep it is. Now I'd like you to gather in groups of three. Willie, you can invite one of the kids to join your group."

There was a bit of shuffling around as the kids chose friends who would make up their groups. The instructors all introduced themselves to their chosen group. All of the students, including Sam, wore life vests. Charlie and Sally introduced themselves to each group, since they would be working with all of them.

"Okay, kids," said Ted, "I'm going to let Paul talk to you before we start. Paul is a Canadian champion swimmer. He has many medals and trophies that he's won for long distance swimming, some of them from when he was as young as you, and he'll give you some tips on how to be a really good swimmer."

"Hi, kids," said Paul. "The first thing we're going to do is some breathing exercises. Breathing properly when you're swimming helps you to relax. It also keeps you from panicking. People who panic usually stop breathing. That's why some people drown, so on my count of one, take a deep breath. Breathe out on two, breathe in on three, and out on four. Are you ready? One, breathe in … two, out … three, in … four, out. That's pretty good. Now let's do that again a couple more times."

They breathed in and out to Paul's count, and their teachers did the exercise as well to keep them on an even rhythm.

"Very good," Paul praised them. "Now you have to learn to breathe and use your arms and kick all at the same time. We're going to begin your lessons with the breast stroke. We'll try that first, combining it with your breathing, like this." He demonstrated. "You see how I breathed in and out in one sweep. Breathe in as you reach out in front of you, and out as you sweep your arms around to the side. Then breathe in again as you reach out to the front, and out as you sweep in an arc to the side, and repeat. Let's try that."

The teachers did the exercise along with their three students and helped those who were unable to breathe and stroke at the same time. They worked on this for about twenty minutes. Some kids got it, but some would need special attention.

Willie and Sam were good students. It was a mission for them. They wanted to learn all they could from these expert swimmers, and they didn't joke around like some of the kids. Ted was surprised that Willie was able to contain his excitement and concentrate on the importance of breathing properly in combination with the exercise.

A couple of the boys were unruly. Everything was a joke for them. Finally, Paul separated them and brought one of them, Barney, whom he felt was the instigator, into his own class, and moved Johnny, who was working hard to get it right, to Barney's original place with Peggy. When no one was interested in joking with Barney, he settled down and began to do the work.

"You're doing a great job, kids," Paul praised them. "You'll need to practice that even when you're not in the water. Now we're coming to the hard part. If you think it was difficult to remember to breathe properly while you do the breast stroke, then you're going to think this next exercise is really hard. But if you practice even in your bed, it will make you a better swimmer. Once you get this next exercise in coordination with the first two, we'll try them out in the water. How does that sound?"

"Yeah!" The kids were jubilant and ready to continue.

"Okay, kids! Let's settle down so we can continue. Now I want you to sit on the ground, and we'll practice the first two exercises. At the same time, we'll be kicking the legs like this," and he demonstrated for them. "When you sweep your arms around, you kick at the same time, and don't forget to breathe."

Sally and Charlie moved around from group to group, and when they saw a kid who was having trouble, they sat down with him and helped him to coordinate the exercise. After about fifteen minutes of this, Paul called the kids all together.

"Don't forget, when you aren't in the water, practice these three exercises together, and you'll find that within a very short time, you'll be really fine swimmers. If you don't practice, you'll be weak swimmers. It's as simple as that.

"Now we're going to try these lessons out in the water. Keep your life vests on until your teachers tell you to take them off. I want you to get used to combining these three principals before you try without the vests. Once you get the rhythm, you'll be like little frogs in the water. Let's go."

Andy and the two police officers sat back and watched as Paul prepared the kids for the water.

"That guy knows what he's talking about," said Officer Cliff. "These exercises before they go in the water will give them more confidence. Most kids dog paddle first and swallow a lot of water. Getting lessons from a champion swimmer and certified divers would give any kid more confidence in the water. My dad threw me in the deep end and terrified me when I was eight years old. I wish I'd had this kind of instruction when I was a kid. I've always been afraid of the water."

"You can't swim then, Cliff?" asked Andy.

"Not very well. I do a terrified dog paddle, but I hope I never have to save anybody in the water."

"Then maybe you should take these classes," Andy suggested. "You've watched the exercises, and you'd never get another chance like this to learn the right way. One more is not going to make a difference to them."

"Oh, they wouldn't teach an old codger like me," said Cliff.

"There's another man here called Sam," Andy told him. "They saved his and his boy's life at Slocan Lake in B.C. He said he was drowning, and Paul dove down twelve feet to save him and bring him up to the surface. The only thing holding his twelve-year-old son up was a life vest. They're both thankful they didn't die, and they're learning to swim the proper way."

Cliff scratched his chin as he considered what Andy was saying. "How long are they going to be here?" he asked.

"I'm not sure, but I think till the end of the week. When they offered to take the place of my missing swim coach, I told them they could camp here for free. In your line of work, you never know when you'd have to go into the water after a kid or anyone for that matter. I'd ask Paul or Ted if I were you."

"Hmm … I just might do that. I've always felt like a real fool in the water doing the dog paddle and afraid I was going to drown, while little kids could swim around me like fish."

"Look, Cliff," Andy pointed. "They're in the water, and they're doing the exercises they've been taught. It's their first time, but they're doing great."

"Yeah, I can see that. I'll talk to Paul when he has a break," said Cliff.

The kids really were doing great. Little Pricilla was probably ten years old, and Johnny looked about eight. They managed the breast stroke and the kick like they'd been doing it for years. No one was more surprised than they were. Sam and Willie did a twelve-stroke lap without having to stop and rest. When they stopped, they treaded water in place as Ted had shown them.

"I can swim, Dad," Willie shouted.

"Well, we've made a good start of it," his dad said. "We'll see what happens when we take off the vests. But for now, I'm happy we've been swimming, even if it's with a life vest. I'm feeling pretty good about this."

Holly had two little nine-year-old girls called Ginny and Symara, and an eleven-year-old boy called Ben. They listened to everything Holly told them, and when she showed them how they could stretch when they reached forward with their arms, they worked really hard to please her. They would definitely be swimming in no time.

Bonnie was having a problem with one uncoordinated boy named Ronnie. The two girls, Sylvia and Kylie, were doing fine, but Ronnie couldn't seem to synchronize the breathing, breast stroke, and kicking.

He was trying his best, but Bonnie remembered how her little brother had trouble learning to do the same thing, so she asked Sally to spend a little time with him while she worked with the two girls.

Peggy and Laurie were making great progress. Johnny was Peggy's prize pupil. He was doing so well that the other two, a boy named Daylen and a girl named Candace, tried to out-do him, and Peggy told them they would probably be swim team champions one day. This was high praise, because Peggy didn't pass out praise very often.

Laurie's three students, Jane, Sarah, and Evan, were really proud of themselves and were hoping their parents were watching, which of course they were. They made their presence known by waving at their children every time they happened to look their way. Evan challenged the girls to a race, and Laurie encouraged them to go for it. Sarah won, and Evan came in last, but it didn't seem to bother him. He was happy because he was swimming.

Paul decided to call a break. The kids had been working pretty hard, and they had made a lot of progress.

"Okay, kids, we're going to take a break. You've got fifteen minutes. When you come back, we're going to take off the life vests and see how much you've learned. Don't worry, we won't let anybody drown, and we won't be in deep water. You can have a drink, but you can't eat. That's something we'll talk about later. You can't eat while you're swimming."

The kids scattered to find their parents, and they didn't seem to be too worried about giving up their life vests. It was evident they trusted their teachers. Officer Cliff decided at that moment to talk to Paul and Ted, so he approached them as they sat down at a picnic table. He hoped they would fit him into the class.

"Hi there, guys. I'm really impressed with how you and your friends handled so many children. I watched all the exercises and realized my father didn't know anything about teaching kids to swim when he threw me into the deep end of the pool when I was eight years old. I've been terrified of the water ever since, so I was wondering if you could fit me into your class."

"Absolutely," said Paul. "Do you not swim at all?"

"Just a panicked dog paddle. But like Andy pointed out to me, in my job, I might be called on to fish a kid, or someone else, out of the water, and with all I know about swimming, I would probably drown us both if I tried."

"With a dog paddle, you probably would," said Paul. "You've been watching the exercises. If you practice them at home till you can synchronize your breathing, breast stroke, and kick, you can begin tomorrow morning at ten o'clock. I'll fit you into my class. I started the kids out with the breast stroke because they need to learn to breathe, but I'll be introducing the Australian crawl, probably on Thursday. You need to know how to do both.

"Bring a life vest for your first lesson." Paul continued. "When you manage the combination, you'll be able to swim without it."

"Thank you," said Cliff. "I'll be here. Okay if I just watch the rest of the lesson today? I don't have a swim suit or life vest with me, and I'm on call, but I'll book off tomorrow morning."

"Sure. Try to remember everything you see me teach. There's another man in Ted's class named Sam. He couldn't swim at all, and he's doing very well. At least you can dog paddle, so you'll learn quickly."

"I hope so," said Cliff. "It's a very bad dog paddle."

"That's okay," Paul assured him. "You've got a head start on those who can't swim at all."

Just then, Holly arrived with a tray of juice and water and passed an orange juice to the guys.

"There's some for you too, Officer Cliff," she said as she handed him an orange juice in a paper cup.

"Thank you, Holly."

"I wanted to ask you something, Officer Cliff. Do you know what happened to the missing coach? Don't you think it's strange that she didn't show up, or that she didn't call to cancel? If she had an accident, you would know, wouldn't you?"

"Yes, I would assume so," he said, "but she hasn't been missing twenty-four hours yet. She might show up within that time. If not, we'll put out an APB on her and start looking."

The kids began to trickle back, and Paul called the classes together.

They'd all taken their vests off and were excited to see if their exercises had paid off. Only the adults were nervous. The kids seemed to have great faith in their coaches, and they looked on Paul like he was a movie star.

The students didn't seem nervous as they entered the water to join their individual classes with their coaches. Their teachers led them out to where the water was just touching their chests. As long as they could feel their feet under them, they weren't afraid, and they trusted their teachers. The coaches demonstrated as they lowered themselves into the water, taking a deep breath as they swept their arms around and kicked their feet.

"Now," said Paul, "your teachers will help you, one at a time, to take the first few strokes. The others will wait their turn, and then the teachers will help them. Just don't be impatient."

Willie was chomping at the bit to get going, but he waited till Ted pointed to him.

"Okay, Willie," Ted said. "Let's see if you've been listening to Paul. Are you ready?"

"I sure am, Ted. Let's go." Willie began his breathing exercise. Reaching out in front of him, he started the sweep and kick, and he was off.

"Keep breathing in and out, Willie. You're doing great," Ted encouraged him.

"Look at him go," Sam shouted. "I can't believe it."

"You can do that too, Sam," said Ted. "Barney's next. Are you ready, Barney?"

"Yes, Ted. Will I be able to swim like Willie?" he asked. "He's sure doin' good."

"Absolutely! Just remember to breathe, sweep, and kick the way you've been practicing. Okay, go!"

Barney put his hands together and reached out into a sweep as he breathed in and out, at the same time kicking like a mule. He seemed very surprised that he didn't sink. Now Willie and Barney were like little frogs in the water, and it was Sam's turn. The look on his face told Ted he was fearful. Maybe it was because he was afraid he'd make a fool of himself in front of Willie. *I'm a big man*, he thought. *Surely, I will sink.*

"I don't think I can do it, Ted," said Sam.

"Yes, you can," Ted coaxed him. "Let's go out to where the water's up to your chest. There won't be enough water for you to drown in, and I'll be with you. We saved you before, so trust me enough to guarantee you won't drown. Willie and Barney are okay, so let's go, Sam."

Ted led the way, and Sam reluctantly followed till they reached the right depth. Ted then demonstrated.

"Okay, Sam, you did the exercise perfectly with the life vest on. Do it like that, and I guarantee you won't sink. Breathe in, reach out, sweep your arms, and don't forget to kick. Ready?"

Sam nodded "yes," and Ted said, "Okay, go!"

Sam put his hands together like he was praying and took the plunge. He remembered to breathe as he reached out and swept his arms around in the breast stroke, kicking in perfect time, and he was swimming. No one was more surprised than Sam.

"You did it, Sam," Ted shouted. "Keep it up. You're strong, and you'll be a great swimmer."

All the little kids were swimming now. Their parents were elated. Some of them were laughing, and some were crying … probably because most of them couldn't swim themselves. It always amazed Holly and her friends how adults who couldn't swim would take their little children to vacation by the water. When the children got into trouble in the water, the parents were unable to save them.

As a lifeguard, Paul had saved dozens of little kids while their parents stood helplessly on the shore, or river bank, completely traumatized with feelings of utter despair. It gave some of them the incentive to learn to swim, but not all. Holly's team, the intrepid foursome, had saved both adults and children. That's why they felt it a privilege to teach this class of children and fill in for the missing coach.

They called an end to the lesson at twelve o'clock. The kids had half an hour of exercises and an hour and fifteen minutes in the water. It was enough for the first day. The RCMP officers were still there, and they were amazed at the kids' progress after only one lesson. Paul told the students to practice in shallow water and to be ready tomorrow morning at ten o'clock for their next lesson.

"That's very good of you," said Andy. "I didn't expect you to offer any more of your vacation time for the kids. Thank you very much."

"We're going to be here anyway," said Holly, "and tomorrow will just be a one hour lesson. Our team has talked it over, and we'll donate one hour each day while we're here, so the kids can feel safe in the water."

"Thank you," said Andy. "We did promise the campers we'd have a swim coach this week. I don't know why she didn't show up, but I think she might have had a problem handling this many kids by herself."

"Yes, I've been thinking about that," said Holly. "With so many of us teaching, the kids had more one on one instruction, but I'm concerned about your coach. My father's a detective, and he's camping in Blairmore. Do you mind if I ask him to look into the disappearance?"

"A detective you say? Do you think he would?" Andy asked. "We don't have a detective in the Pass."

"I'm sure he would. I also wanted to ask you if you had any other scuba divers staying at the camp. When we were diving on the sunken railway cars yesterday, we saw a scuba diver. He turned and headed across the lake when he saw us. The way he took off made me think he didn't want to be seen. He was alone, and scuba divers aren't supposed to dive without a buddy, so there probably is another diver in the area."

"I was thinking about your missing canoes," she said. "The thieves could have easily moved them across the lake using the paddles. If they did that, they wouldn't be heard, and the items that were stolen would fit easily into two canoes with only one person paddling in each."

Officer Cliff was listening with interest to Holly's suggestion. "That's very good thinking," he said. "I never even thought of that scenario, but it's certainly possible. We're short- staffed at the station, since it's vacation time. Maybe I'll stop in at the Blairmore camp and have a chat with your father. He might have some suggestions about our missing swim coach as well. Did anyone ever tell you that you think like a detective?"

"All the time," said Holly. "My team has helped my father solve some of his cases, especially when teenagers are involved."

"Is that so? Well, I'm looking forward to tomorrow morning's lessons. It's been great meeting you all. Have a nice holiday."

Andy showed them where they could set up their tents and where the facilities were.

"You're welcome to join us for lunch," said Andy. "There's always plenty of food."

"Thanks, Andy," said Holly, "but we have lots of food with us, and we'll be joining our parents at the other camp tonight for dinner. It's going to be a catered affair to celebrate our family reunion, so we'd better be there. Thanks for the offer, though. Okay, guys, let's choose a picnic table and have lunch. The cave and railway cars are waiting for us."

Holly got her duffle bag cooler from the trunk of Peggy's car, and Bonnie helped to lay the table. She spread the pretty, flowered picnic tablecloth over the table, and Holly set out paper plates and plastic cutlery. Then she set out plastic bowls of chicken, potato salad, macaroni salad, and mixed garden salad, as well as a large bottle of juice, bottled water, and two kinds of pie (apple and lemon meringue).

Andy happened to walk over to pick up some lawn chairs and saw the spread on the picnic table.

"No wonder you didn't want to join us for lunch. I'd rather eat here too."

"Holly's duffle bag is pure magic," said Paul. "She's the queen of the caterers."

"Actually, it's my mother who's the queen of the culinary arts. She keeps the fridge stocked so that I can feed my friends. Okay, guys, let's give thanks for the food, and then we can eat."

Holly said grace, and Andy walked into the hall with a smile on his face. "Nice kids," he said to his wife, Sheila.

The Cave

THE GROUP OF YOUNG SCUBA DIVERS PARKED AT THE OTHER END OF THE LAKE and saw that only one trailer remained there now. A man was fishing from the river bank, and he waved a greeting to the group. Further back along the river stood some privately-owned cabins and a number of very nice year-round homes.

A bridge spanned the river, and the fast water rushed over the rocks and into the lake. At this point the lake was very cold, but the fishing was good. Lake trout and rainbow trout were in abundance. Even though the water was cold, two young boys from the trailer were swimming, and the cold didn't seem to bother them.

The trek to the cave didn't seem so far this time. It was a beautiful sunny day, and the group followed the railway tracks till they reached the area just below the cave.

"I'm not going in there until the guys go in with beaters to roust out anything that might be dwelling in the shadows," said Bonnie.

The girls all agreed. The fright with the colony of bats flying at their heads was not something they would easily forget. Paul and Ted got their zoom flashlights and armed themselves with a couple of spear guns, just in case they ran into a wild animal interested in eating them—at least that was what Ted said, with a huge grin. This was more to appease the girls than anything else, and off they went into the black hole. Charlie waited with the girls. While they waited for Paul and Ted to return, they put on their scuba gear over their swim wear. They each wore a helmet with a lantern attached. Ted would carry the floodlight, since he was the biggest and strongest, and Paul would carry other things, such as rope and cameras.

The guys were back in ten minutes or so. They assured the girls the bats were gone and that there were no other scary animals that they could see.

"The tunnel is low for about twenty feet," said Paul, "but it gets wider and opens up to about seven feet in height. I need the floodlight to see what's ahead. The good news is that the water recedes as we go forward, and I think it will trickle off."

"It's good you're wearing your scuba gear," said Ted, "because we don't know what we're going to find. It looks very interesting, though. We'd better gear up, Paul."

In a few minutes they were ready to go. Ted hoisted the floodlight onto his shoulder to keep it clear of the water. Paul had two ropes wrapped around him and was carrying a movie camera on his shoulder. Both guys had waterproof bags slung over their shoulders, and they took the lead lighting the way.

Holly's team had explored caves before; however, even though they were experienced, they approached each new venture with a certain amount of trepidation. The novices were understandably nervous.

The water came up to their armpits at the beginning, and they were able to swim for approximately twenty feet before it gradually depleted to a depth of three feet or less. Now they were sloshing through on foot, but they discovered that as they proceeded forward, the water was becoming less and less until it was just a trickle.

Paul unwound one of the ropes he had wrapped around himself and told the others to each make a loop about four feet apart and slip the loop around their left wrists. They would need three or four feet between each of them to give them room to move. There was fifty feet of rope, plenty for the task, and it would protect them from getting lost and also give them support from the others in case of an accident.

"There might be some crevasses," he warned, "and since we don't know what's up ahead, if we're attached to each other, we should most likely be able to handle any situation. It's just a precaution."

The young explorers did as Paul suggested and were soon on their way again. So far nobody was complaining. There was an air of excitement among them. The walls and floor of the cave were of solid rock, and as they proceeded forward, the tunnel got wider and suddenly opened up to a huge chamber.

"Wow!" they all exclaimed at once. Ted shone the floodlight around the cavern walls, and Paul, Holly, and Bonnie shone their zoom flashlights into the wall's crevices.

"Look at this," said Holly. "There's native art work on the walls, just like we found in the Lyndaman Island caves. I still want to know how they did this without light."

"They must have had torches, like the professor suggested," said Ted. "But how would they have brought the light in here?"

"Possibly the same way we did," said Holly, "but they probably used fish oil and wicks."

"Hey, I've found another tunnel," said Magen. "Oh, and here's another one." She was shining her zoom flashlight around the walls. Are we going to explore these as well?"

"I don't know why not," said Paul, "but I think we should be very cautious. I wonder how many people have been this far into the cave. Do you know, Peggy or Laurie?"

"If they have, I've never heard of it," said Laurie. "I think the water at the entrance would have been a deterrent, and I haven't heard of anybody at the Pass with the equipment, such as floodlighting and movie cameras, or even the interest, in exploring any further than the entrance."

"Neither have I," said Peggy. "Also, bats and the low ceiling entrance might've changed anyone's mind about delving into the blackness of the cave. It's only recently that scuba divers have shown any interest in diving to find the railway cars. I think Laurie, Dad, and I are the only scuba divers in the Pass."

"I wonder if the professor has ever been in here," said Ted. "He seems to know this area really well. We'll have to ask him this evening when we go for dinner."

"I heard Dad say that he and Uncle Gordon spent a lot of time here when they were young," said Peggy. "Dad said that's when he fell in love with the area and decided to move here."

"Well, I think we should try to find out more about the cave before we check out the tunnels," said Ted. "We want to go see the Frank Slide tomorrow. The Interpretive Centre will have all kinds of information, so I think we should wait."

"Okay," said Paul, "but since we have the floodlight with us, what do you say if you and I take a quick look just a few feet beyond the entrance?"

"Well, maybe a few feet," said Ted. "The rest of you stay here while Paul and I check one of the tunnels out."

"Don't worry about us," said Holly. "We'll be fine. Our atomic zoom flashlights will give us plenty of light, and we can check the art work on the walls while you're gone. I'm glad Bonnie and I brought our cameras. We can take some pictures. Just don't be too long."

"Yeah," said Charlie. "Don't be too long. It feels like a crypt in here … kind of creepy."

"Oh, don't be such a wuss," said Sally. "I find this thrilling. It's like going back in time."

The girls all agreed, so Charlie was outnumbered; he decided to keep his thoughts to himself. Paul and Ted were already in the tunnel, and the girls were ecstatic about their find. The stalactites hanging from the ceiling of the chamber, and the stalagmites on the floor, formed their own natural art work and gave an eerie, haunted look to the place— much like the staging of an enchanted mystery movie.

"We would have heard about this if others had been in here," said Peggy. "Small towns are known for their gossip, and this would never have been kept secret. I think we're the only people who've been here, at least since ancient times. Wait until we get around the fire tonight. Do we have a story to tell? I think we do!"

"Look at the picture of this totem," said Holly. "The colours are so vivid. I wonder what they used for what we call paint. Ordinary paint today wouldn't hold the colour like that. It would have faded away over time, but this colour is bright and looks fresh. And how many eons has it been in the dark?"

"You're right," said Bonnie. "Look at this painting of a pheasant. It's so beautiful, and it's hidden away." She was snapping pictures as she spoke. "And here's a picture of a young native boy holding a robin so tenderly, and it's not afraid. It's quite content to sit in his hand."

"This reminds me of the paintings in the pharaoh's tombs," said Holly. "The colours on those paintings are pristine after thousands of years. I don't think we have paint like that today."

The girls' excitement began to rub off on Charlie, and he started to take an interest in this incredible discovery. He ran the beam of his flashlight along the walls and floor, and he thought he saw something white. His curiosity got the better of him, so he followed the beam of his light over to the far wall.

There was something on the floor. He bent over to take a closer look and discovered it was a piece of what looked like a white bone-shaped knife. There was a point on it and a carved handle. Charlie picked it up, and he suddenly realized he had found what looked like an ancient weapon.

"Hey," he shouted. "Look what I found. I think it's an ancient knife. It looks very old, and it's made of bone."

The girls rushed over, and they each wanted to hold it.

"I think you've made a real find," said Holly. "I wonder if there are any other artifacts to be found. We'll ask Ted when he comes out of the tunnel what he thinks. Ted's a professional tracker, and he's found some interesting native weapons."

"I wonder if it's worth anything," said Charlie.

"Ted could tell you," said Holly. "I wonder what's keeping him and Paul. They said they would only be ten minutes, but it's been at least twenty minutes or more. I hope they're okay. If they aren't back in five more minutes, I'll start to worry."

There was no sound from the tunnel, and now the rest of the kids were beginning to feel as anxious as Holly. They each shone their zoom flashlights into the blackness of the tunnel, hoping to see some sign of the two guys, but to no avail. Holly and Bonnie called out to them, but they didn't get an answer.

"They told us to wait here," said Holly. "I wonder if Bonnie and I should go in and search for them. The tunnel doesn't seem to be more than four and a half feet high, at least at the entrance. We might not be able to stand up straight. It would be even tougher for the guys, as they are taller than we are, especially Ted. He's about six feet. Paul's about five nine."

"Let's wait a few more minutes," said Bonnie. "If the tunnel is really small and the guys are coming this way, there may not be room for us to turn around, and we could get stuck."

"You're right, of course," said Holly, "but if they don't show up soon, we should get out of here and phone Daddy and the professor for help. I feel responsible, because I'm the one who always wants to take the risks, and I shouldn't involve new divers like Sally and Charlie, since they're underage."

"You shouldn't feel responsible for Charlie and me," said Sally. "After all, we'll be eighteen next month, and we've been known to take a few risks in our lives. My mother says we live a charmed life because of our choices and the fact that we've always managed to stay safe. We do our best to be responsible."

"I see a light," Peggy shouted. She shone her flashlight into the tunnel. "It's a long way back, but it's coming this way."

A cheer went up from the group, and they took turns shining their flashlights into the tunnel. They all crowded around the entrance and shouted encouragement as the light advanced slowly towards them. It was obvious that progress was slow, probably because of the low ceiling.

Paul and Ted finally reached the exit and burst through to exultant cheers from their comrades. They were bent over like old men, and it took them awhile before they could straighten up to face their friends.

"Are you okay?" Holly asked. "We were so worried when you didn't come back in ten minutes." She tried to give Paul a hug, but he was still trying to straighten his back.

"I will be, when I work out the kinks in my back," he told her. "Wait till we tell you what we found."

"Oh, your poor back," Holly said as she massaged his shoulders and upper back. He groaned as she rubbed his neck.

Bonnie did the same for Ted.

"Oh, you don't know how good that feels," Ted moaned. "The reason we didn't come back in ten minutes," he said between moans and groans, "is because it was a one-way street in there. There wasn't room to turn around with the floodlight and cameras, so we had to keep going and hope for a pull out. The ceiling was so low, we couldn't walk upright, and sometimes we had to crawl."

"Yeah," Paul agreed. "I couldn't complain, because Ted is so much bigger than me, and he was carrying the floodlight. It had to be excruciating for him. Thank God we had the light, though, because we did come to another chamber."

"Another chamber?" They were all shouting at once.

"Yes," said Ted, "but there's no way we'll want to go back in there."

"Why not? What did you find?" Holly asked excitedly.

"It was a burial crypt," said Ted. "There were about thirty skeletons in there, wrapped up like mummies and all laid out in neat rows. How they got them in there, I'll never know, but they must have been there for centuries."

"Wow! I said it was like a crypt," Charlie said. The girls looked shocked. "Was there anything else there?"

"What else would be in a burial chamber?" Paul asked.

"Well, Charlie found something here in this chamber," said Holly. "Show it to Paul and Ted, Charlie."

Charlie showed them his treasure, and Ted's face lit up when he saw it. "Cool, Charlie. That's a real nice piece. Where did you find it?"

Charlie showed him, and Ted turned the floodlight and shone it back and forth along the wall. There was a little alcove just above the spot where the knife was found, and Ted ran his hand along the top of it.

"I think there's something here," he said. "Here, Paul, hold the floodlight for me and shine it on this spot."

Paul held the floodlight above his head and aimed the beam at the alcove while Ted reached into a hole in the rock about a foot above his head and pulled out a buckskin pouch.

"What is it?" Charlie exclaimed.

"We'll know in a minute," Ted said as he pulled a buckskin tie apart and emptied the contents on the ground.

The pouch was quite large and well preserved, and it contained an interesting variety of ancient weapons, such as hand carved knives, sharp metal pieces, precious stones, a vest, and a pair of buckskin slippers. There was also a piece of wood, about twelve inches long, carved like a totem and painted in bright colours.

"Cool," said Charlie. "What are these little metal pieces?"

"They look like primitive arrow heads," said Ted. "I think this is a warrior's pouch. It's filled with all kinds of items like charms and things that a warrior would take with him on a hunt or a journey. It's a real nice find. I wonder how old it is. Maybe the professor would know."

"We can ask him tonight when we go for dinner," said Holly. "I'm sure he and Daddy will want to see the inside of the cave, though I don't think they'll want to make the trip through the tunnel to the crypt."

"I wouldn't blame them," said Peggy. "I know I don't want to go. I'm not interested in disturbing the dead. The local folk always thought this cave was creepy."

"That's how I feel," said Bonnie, and the other girls all agreed. Charlie decided to keep quiet. If truth be told, burrowing into a hole like a mole wasn't his idea of fun.

"Let's get out of here," said Bonnie. "We've got lots of pictures to show Detective Brannigan and the professor. There's still time for us to check out the railway cars."

"You're right," said Ted. He put the pouch into his waterproof bag and sealed it. "We'll discuss the contents of the pouch later. Okay, guys, let's go."

"We won't need the rope, since we know the way," said Paul. "Just keep your headlamps on and stay close."

There were no mishaps on the way. They stayed close together as they swam through the tunnel, and the feelings of trepidation the group had felt on entering the cave had evaporated, but they were glad to see the sunlight at the exit. Paul, Charlie, and the girls were able to swim through the tunnel, because their cameras were underwater models.

Ted, however, had to walk through four feet of water as he held the floodlight over his head. They gave a cheer as they exited the cave, and when they climbed down the bank to the water's edge, Ted left the floodlight and pouch behind a rock and covered them with branches, hoping the thieves who robbed the camp were not in the vicinity. He would use an underwater camera like the others, and he was also equipped with an underwater headlamp and underwater-zoom-atomic-flashlight, like the rest of the group.

They all slipped into the water, staying close to their buddies, and paid close attention to their leaders. When they neared the site of the sunken railway cars, they suddenly became aware that two other divers were already at the wrecks. The two divers were busy taking pictures and hadn't noticed they had company until Ted and the young dive team were practically beside them.

Paul and Ted signaled hello to them, but the other two made unfriendly, obscene, gestures and then suddenly turned and swam away as fast as they could, heading in the direction of the far bank. Ted gave the signal to surface, and they all ascended to the top. There was an air of surprise on each face.

"Well, what do you think guys?" said Ted. "Are you thinking what I'm thinking?"

"Yeah," said Paul, "I think there's something suspicious about those guys."

"I don't get it," said Peggy. "People around here pride themselves on being friendly to visitors. Those two can't be from here. They certainly didn't want to meet us."

"Well, I'm thinking they might be the robbers," said Holly. "Remember what I said about how scuba divers could swim in and steal the canoes and load the other items into them and paddle away without being heard? Maybe these are the culprits. They certainly don't want to be seen; otherwise, why would they behave the way they did, and why take off like they were doing something wrong?"

"Maybe we should call it a day," said Holly, "and give Officer Cliff a call. We can dive on the railway cars before we go home. What do you think?"

"I'm with you," said Paul. "What do you say, guys?"

The others all agreed, and they decided to go to the camp and give Andy a heads up. At Paul's signal, they descended for the swim back to the cave to retrieve the floodlight and buckskin pouch. Ted would have to walk back to the car and bikes because of the floodlight, but the others would swim.

Ted was a tracker and didn't mind the trek. He loved to hike, and his long legs took him there almost as fast as the scuba divers. When they shed their scuba gear and were dressed and ready to go, they headed to the other end of the lake and arrived at the camp just as the children were getting together on benches. Andy had his guitar out. He welcomed the young divers and asked if they would like to join them in a sing-along.

"We sure would," said Holly. "But before we do, we need to tell you that there are two hostile scuba divers in the lake. We called Officer Cliff and told him. Maybe they aren't the robbers, but we wanted the police to know they're here, and they're behaving in a very suspicious manner."

She told Andy what had happened, and he said it did sound suspicious. He told them the same thing Peggy had ... that people around the Pass were friendly.

"When the scuba divers were here before to dive on the railway cars and take pictures, they were great," he said. "There were no complaints about them from anybody. These two might be a couple of bad boys. I'm glad you phoned Cliff, what with the robbery and everything. He'll look into it."

"That's good," said Holly, "so we're going to sing, are we? Well, let's get our instruments, and we'll help you out."

"Maybe you don't know the songs we sing," said Andy.

"I bet we do. You name them, and we'll play them. Okay, guys, let's get our instruments."

They had the instruments out in two minutes.

"Do you have a keyboard?" Bonnie asked.

"Yes, indeed we do. Hey, Danny!" he shouted. "Bring out the keyboard. Can you play?" he asked Bonnie.

"Yes, sir!" Bonnie said as she ran to help Danny set the keyboard up. She quickly found a place to plug it in.

The others were ready in about ten minutes. Holly ran a few chords up and down the accordion while Bonnie followed her on the keyboard. Ted, as usual, took over the mic that somebody had set up.

"We take requests," he said. "Who's first? What would you like to sing?"

"'This Little Light of Mine,'" little Pricilla suggested.

Holly gave them an intro on the accordion, and Ted led them into the chorus. Bonnie played the keyboard, and Peggy and Laurie joined Paul and Andy on their guitars. Charlie had found Ted's bongo drum, and he beat out a pretty fine rhythm. Magen and Sally joined Ted at the mic and harmonized along with Holly, Paul, and Bonnie.

Andy thought he'd died and gone straight to heaven. For a week that had started out with nothing but trouble, he thought God had intervened and sent him nine angels. The kids threw chorus after chorus at them, and they not only knew them, but they played and sang them like they'd been practicing for a week. Andy wore a grin a mile wide.

When they asked for another request, Andy said, "Would you sing something that you'd like to sing?"

"Your wish is our command," said Holly. "We're very fortunate to have someone who sings with the voice of an angel, so Ted will sing and we'll back him."

Bonnie and Holly caressed the keys with the intro for "Hallelujah," and Ted began to sing. Paul strummed lightly on the guitar, and Holly and Bonnie sang in a harmony that was so soft and sweet, it was like the birds were singing in the trees. Ted's voice soared upward, and they soared with him to a crescendo that brought tears to Andy's eyes.

"Bravo," he shouted, and he applauded so hard his hands were hurting. The staff and all the adult campers were applauding with him and shouting, "Bravo! Bravo! Bravo!"

"I'd never have believed it—that you could know and play every chorus the kids like to sing, but to have so much talent arrive on our doorstep when this week had started so badly, it's like a gift from God. You filled in as swim coaches, and now to give us a concert like this. It's more than we could ever hope or dream of. God is good!"

Holly noticed Officer Cliff standing at the back of the audience. He'd been applauding along with the others, and then he approached Andy and the dive team accompanied by his deputy, Officer Roland.

"Wow, folks! That was a great concert you gave the little kids," he said. "You really lucked out here today, Andy, in spite of your other problems."

"Right, Cliff. And on top of that, they may have figured out how the thieves were able to abscond with the goods without making a noise."

"Yeah, they told us, but now they say they saw another scuba diver at the railway car site. Two of them. That makes sense. It would require two people to load and remove the two canoes as silently as they did."

"You should get a guard dog, Andy," said Holly. "If anyone came around at night, the dog would wake up the whole camp."

"I've thought of it," he answered, "but I'm afraid the dog might hurt the children."

"Not if you get the right dog," said Holly. "Our friend, the professor, has a dog named Socrates. He loves children, but he also knows the difference between friend and foe. If someone was sneaking around here in the middle of the night, he would raise such a ruckus, you'd definitely hear him. And he'd probably attack and hold at least one of the thieves till you appeared.

"If you catch one, it's possible you'll find out who the other one is. He wouldn't hurt the thief, but there's no way the guy would get away. The worst that would happen to him is that he'd be held down and might get licked to death, but I guarantee the miscreant would be scared to death."

"That's probably a very good idea," Andy agreed. "We've always said no pets allowed, but it's something to think about."

"If you like, we could borrow Socrates from the professor for the time we're here," said Holly. "He's very gentle with children, and they'd love him. He's not so gentle if he doesn't like you, and he's a very good judge of character. He'd guard the camp and the children like they were his own. It would give you an idea whether you want a dog or not. If you decide you don't want him around, we can take him back to the other camp."

"I'll ask the campers what they think of the idea," said Andy, "and if they agree, we could try it."

"Cool," said Paul. "Do you happen to know if any other divers or locals have explored the cave?"

"I haven't heard if anyone has gone in past the entrance," said Andy. "I just heard there's a lot of water in the cave, and the tunnel is so low and dark that nobody is interested in taking the plunge. They're afraid they might get trapped in there."

"Then you probably don't know that many centuries ago it was used as a burial crypt, probably by the aboriginals, and they painted beautiful pictures on the walls."

"No, I didn't know that. How could they paint pictures? Wouldn't it be dark in there? And how would they get the bodies in there to bury them?"

"That's what we want to find out," said Ted. "This is the reason we scuba dive—to search for past history. Our friend, the professor, is a historian. He's a master scuba diver and knows this area, but I don't think he knows about this. Who do you think he should talk to? Is there anyone in the Pass who's a native historian?"

"Old Chief George is the oldest native I know. He's from the Blackfoot tribe, and he lives in a cabin at the foot of Turtle Mountain. He knows more about Aboriginal history than anyone around here. I don't know how old he is, but he must be around a hundred or so."

"Do you think he'd talk to us?" Holly asked.

"Oh, he loves to talk. He was born here, and he was here when the natives were fighting over this land with the coal companies. He'd be delighted to talk to anyone who wants to know about the past. History gets buried over the years when prosperity takes over. Nobody wants to remember the hard times. Yes, old George would definitely love to talk to you."

"Great!" said Holly. "Can you give us directions to his cabin?"

"Sure can. Just let me get a piece of paper, and I'll draw you a little map. It's easy enough to find." Andy disappeared into the office and reappeared in a few minutes. He drew the directions, starting with the town of Frank. "When you reach the town of Frank, you'll see a sign for Hillcrest. Turn right and follow the road to the first turn-off, and turn right again. About a hundred yards in, you'll see an old cabin in the trees on the left. That's Old Chief's place. He'll talk your ear off. Good luck."

"We're going to see the Frank Slide tomorrow, so we can take in both trips at the same time," said Holly. "Thanks, Andy."

"No, thank you! You've brought some sunshine into our camp and brightened up our day," said Andy with a wide grin.

"Okay, guys, let's go," Holly was itching to get going. "Let's find Daddy and the professor and fill them in on what we've discovered. They should be finished their golf games now. They'll be as excited as we are. We never expected to find what we did in the cave, and they'd want to know about the scuba divers we saw. It's possible they're the thieves who cleaned out the camp and stole the canoes."

The kids climbed on their bikes, and the rest of the group all piled into Peggy's car. The ride into town was uneventful, but it was an excited bunch of young people that joined their parents at the Blairmore campground. The professor's team had won their first round of golf, and Phillip's team had won the second round.

Sam and Kim teamed up with Jeremiah and Lynda. It was a comedy act, since they were not golfers. Their opponents were Molly and Robert Sinclair, and Dennis and Lara. Robert was the only golfer in this group, and he wasn't pleased with the comedic hilarity of the others.

"Oh give it up, Robert," said Molly. "It's just a fun game."

"Just a game?" said Robert. "I thought it was supposed to be a tournament. I was all set to win the gold cup."

"Well, there's no gold cup," said Phillip. "We just wanted to get to know our family again after all these years."

"Oh well, in that case I guess I can forget about the cup. But you're right, it was fun."

"The explorers have arrived," said David. "Did you run into any wild animals or wild people this time?"

"Oh Daddy, wait till you hear what we have to tell you," said Holly excitedly. "This has turned into a terrific vacation."

"I'm all ears. Park yourself here beside me, and the rest of you find a bench and tell us what's got you so excited."

"You won't believe it," she said. "First of all, the camp got robbed. The thieves stole bicycles, camping generators, two 4 HP motors, two canoes, and other small items. And they got away scot free."

"Yes, I heard about it from the RCMP officer. He said he'd met you, and you were helping out at the camp because the swim coach hadn't shown up. I'm glad you were able to help. He consulted with me on the disappearance, since they don't have a detective here at the Pass."

"Were you able to help him? He seems to be stuck," said Holly.

"Well, I tracked her as far as the town of Frank. Apparently, she stopped to view the slide and stopped in at the Interpretative Centre. She signed the visitor's guest book at 4:50 p.m., and Andy had spoken to her earlier when she said she was just leaving Clairsholm, so something must have happened to her after she stopped at the Interpretive Centre. Officers Cliff and Roland are on their way to check out the information, and they said they'd get back to me and let me know what they discover. They'll also find out what kind of car she was driving."

"Oh, I hope she's alright," said Holly. "Maybe she had an accident, but if so, you'd think her car would've been spotted by somebody. Isn't the town of Frank just a few miles down the road?"

"Yes. If the officers don't find her, I think we should get a search party together and search between here and Frank," suggested Ted.

"I agree," said the detective. "Maybe even between the lake and Frank, since she was heading for the lake. I have a bad feeling about this. She'd almost reached her destination when she was at the Interpretative Centre. Well, we'll know more when the RCMP officers return. Also, when we find out what kind of car she was driving, we'll know what we're looking for."

"In the meantime," said the professor, "tell us what you did at the lake."

"Well, you know we taught the little kids how to swim," said Holly. "They were really good too. They caught on really fast, and they listened to everything we tried to teach them. Then we played for their singsong. Andy, the manager, was happy as a lark that we participated, and he told us we could stay there all week for free. By the way, Professor, would you mind lending Socrates to us? We thought he'd make a really good guard dog in case the robbers return."

"Good idea," the professor agreed. "If strangers come around in the middle of the night, he'll raise the camp, and he loves to think he's the boss."

Holly continued with her story of the day's discoveries. "We decided to explore the cave, and you'll never believe what we found."

"Well, hurry up and tell us," said Heather. "We're all ears."

"The entrance to the cave was almost under water. There was about four feet of water, and the tunnel was only about six feet high. Ted had to carry the floodlights on his shoulders, and he had to walk in to protect the lighting equipment. Paul had to carry the cameras and ropes, but he was able to swim, because they were all underwater equipment. The rest of us carried our gear in waterproof backpacks, and we were able to swim in. Poor Ted. He had to bend over because he's so tall, and he was walking through the water."

"That must have been tough, Ted," said the professor compassionately.

"That was nothing," said Ted. "Wait till you hear the rest. Go on, Holly."

"Well, Ted's right," Holly continued. "The tunnel was very confining. Only two could swim side by side, but soon the water receded as we proceeded forward until it was only a trickle and eventually dry. The tunnel walls at this point got wider, and the ceiling higher, so that Ted could straighten up.

"Suddenly, we were in a huge chamber of ebony black rock. It was amazing, and when we shone the lights around the walls, we discovered beautiful native pictures ... the brightest colours you've ever seen, like the ones we found in the Lyndaman Island and Glenmore Mountain caves. Paul and Ted will tell you of the other discoveries."

Paul went on to tell them of the offshoot tunnels and about the one that they almost got stuck in, but when he came to the story about the burial crypt, there was a gasp from the others. No one was more startled than John.

"That's incredible!" he shouted. "I've lived here all my life, and no one's ever told that story, or I would've heard it. That's amazing."

"Don't forget what I discovered," said Charlie, not wanting to be left out of the story. "Don't forget about my ancient bone knife." He took it out of his pocket and displayed it on the table.

"Oh right," said Ted. "I almost forgot. Charlie found a carved native artifact, a knife carved from bone. And I found a pouch of artifacts that probably belonged to a warrior."

Ted pulled the pouch out of his saddle bag and laid the contents out on the ground. The professor carefully studied each of the pieces and Charlie's knife as well while Holly filled everybody in on how the pieces had been found.

"Congratulations, Ted, and you too, Charlie," the professor smiled. "These are real treasures. They'll be a terrific addition to your collection, Ted. I'd like to see your other pieces when we get back home. This is the exciting part of exploring. You never know what you'll find. Do you have any other artifacts, Charlie?"

"No, Uncle Gordon, but I'd like to start a collection, so I'll be looking from now on."

"Well, that knife is a terrific piece to start your collection with," the professor praised him. "Good luck hunting."

David was busy doing research on his phone when he got another bit of news. "Hey, I got another hit on our swim coach's travels. Just before you reach the lake travelling west, there's a tourist information booth. Apparently the swim coach stopped in there just before six o'clock. She introduced herself to the tour guide and said her name was Susannah McCarthy and told him she was going to the camp at the lake to teach swimming to a bunch of kids."

"So she made it to the lake," said Holly. "Where could she have disappeared to? Did he say what she was driving?"

"Yes, as a matter of fact, he did. He said she was driving a sweet little Ford Sport. It was red and brand new. He said she was excited about her new car and told him this was her first trip in it. Now what could have happened to that little girl when she was only a couple of kilometres from her destination?"

David called the RCMP and got Officer Cliff on the phone. He passed the information on to him. They spoke for a few minutes, and

Officer Cliff said he would be right over to talk to him. Meanwhile, Ted was busy organizing a search party.

"We can eat first," said the professor. "We can't start out on empty stomachs and waste all this amazing food. It will be daylight until around ten o'clock. That should give us over three hours of search time. Then we can search again in the morning if we haven't found her."

"We have a class from 10:00 a.m. to 11:00, but we can start early, probably even around 7:00 a.m. We'll take a break for the class at ten, and then continue searching after eleven," said Holly. "Susannah was so close to the camp, it's possible that foul play is involved. Other than an accident, what else could it be?" Now that they had her name, it made it more personal.

A dozen different scenarios were passed around while they ate the marvellous banquet that Phillip and Kate had arranged for them. Meanwhile, the two RCMP officers had arrived, and they were invited to join in the food fest. Ideas were bounced off them, and by the time dinner was over, there was some semblance of preparation and planning so no one would be taking off on their own to try and play the hero.

"I'd like to borrow one of Andy's canoes with a motor," said Paul. "We could take it slowly around the lake to search the banks and bushes. We're not sure what we're looking for, but we don't want to overlook anything. A red car would stand out."

"We've put an APB out on her and the car," said Officer Cliff. "I have to say, this doesn't sound good."

The Search

CHAPTER 6

BY 6:45 P.M., THE SEARCH WAS UNDERWAY. SINCE HOLLY AND HER FRIENDS WERE experienced in search and rescue in the mountains of British Columbia, they consulted with the professor, Detective David Brannigan, and the two RCMP Officers, Cliff and Roland. Holly, Paul, Bonnie, and Ted made up one team, and they helped to set up the other teams by assessing what they could bring to their group to aid in whatever capacity they might be needed.

Before long, they had eight teams of four. Some of the campers joined in on the search. The professor led one team, and David led another. Phillip and John put teams together, and Sam, Jeremiah, and Lawrence each managed to pull enough people in to make teams of four.

The professor and Ted laid out the rules of the search. No one was to go off on his or her own. The RCMP officers would act as floaters, keeping track of each of the teams, and would keep in touch with the professor, Ted, and Detective Brannigan with two way radios. Including the two police officers, this added up to thirty-four people. Each team was given a certain area to cover.

A convoy of cars, bikes, and trucks pulled into the Tourism Information Centre. Since this was the last place Susannah had been seen, the leaders wanted to talk to the young man who had last spoken to her. The man was known to both officers.

He was getting the booth ready to close for the night, locking novelties, maps, and literature away, and basically tidying up.

"Hi, Milton," said Cliff. "Closing for the night I see. Busy day?"

"Not really. How are you, Cliff? Going hiking?"

"I guess you could say that. We just want to ask you a few questions about the young girl with the red car you said was here on Sunday."

"Yeah, I've been thinking about her," said Milton. "The detective said she was missing. Have you not found her yet?"

"No, she's still missing," said Cliff.

"Aw gee, I hope she's okay. She's a nice girl, and she only had another mile or so to go. She said she was going to the camp. Did you talk to Andy?"

"We did. He was the one who reported her missing. She was supposed to be there on Sunday for supper, but she never showed. Andy thought she might have changed her mind about teaching so many kids."

"Oh no, she said she loved kids and was looking forward to it."

"You seem to have had quite a conversation with her," Cliff noted.

"Yeah, I was hoping she was going to be here for a while. I really liked her. In fact, I thought if I got to know her a little better, maybe she'd go out to dinner and a show with me."

"Well, she still might," said Cliff. "We're searching for her."

"How could she get lost between here and the camp?" mused Milton. "If there'd been an accident, I'm sure we'd have heard. There was lots of traffic on Sunday, and she wasn't somebody you'd forget. Can I join you in the search? I know this area like the back of my hand."

"Absolutely! If you're ready to go, we'd appreciate your help."

"I'm ready. Just let me get my jacket and I'll lock up. Is there anything I need to bring with me?"

"Do you have any maps of the trails around here?" Cliff asked. "Some of the searchers aren't from this area, and we don't want anybody getting lost."

"That's something I can supply," said Milton. "Come into the booth and help yourself, Cliff. What area would you be concentrating on?"

"Let me look at your maps, Milton. Professor, you come with me; Ted, you too. You're the trackers, and we're lucky to have Milton here, since he knows the bush country so well and can maybe give us some insight as to where Susannah might be."

"I'm getting a very bad feeling that you think foul play might be involved here," said Milton. "Otherwise, why would she wander off into the bush?"

"We can't rule anything out," said Cliff, "and since the lady has been missing since Sunday, we have to assume something bad may have happened to her. You have a lot of tourists coming to your booth, Milton. Did you happen to notice anything suspicious in the last few days?"

"No, nothing jumps out at me, except … hmm … except for a couple of guys with a motorbike that kept sputtering and stopping. They were so mad I thought they were going to take an ax to it, but they finally got it going and left."

Cliff frowned. "These two guys you saw, were they both on the same bike?"

"Yes," said Milton. "I thought they were going to come to blows because the bike wouldn't start. One kept yelling at the other one that it was a piece of junk, and asked why he picked that one when there were fifty more to choose from. They were scaring off the other tourists, and I was glad when the bike finally started and they left."

"Wait a minute," said Cliff. "We had a call from Jasper's Second Hand Bikes informing us that a bike was stolen off the lot. I wonder if that was the bike. What did these two guys look like?"

"They were both about five feet ten inches in height. One had flaming red hair, and the other one had shoulder length dark hair. The redhead wore a black leather jacket, and the dark one wore a dirty buckskin suede-type jacket."

Cliff phoned it in to the station then told Milton he would be a floater. He owned a trail bike, and would keep an eye on the novice searchers. Each team was given maps and directed to an assigned area.

"Start back for the tourist booth at 9:30 p.m. Don't stay later than that, because it will be dark around 10:00 p.m. We don't want to be searching for you too. It's 7:15 p.m. now, so off you go. If you find anything, get in touch by radio. Each team leader has one."

Holly's team was assigned to the lake area. They borrowed a large canoe from Andy and decided to scan the banks around the edge of the lake. Tomorrow they would search through the trees and dense bushes. Milton had said there were several abandoned derelict cabins along the south side of the lake. They would check those out tomorrow as well.

The weather was cooperating. So far, there had been no rain or fog, and the light breeze was warm and inviting. They could see the kids playing in the water at the camp, and the little 4 HP motor took the canoe through the water like a fish. There were no other boaters on the lake, just one fisherman standing up to his waist in the water on the east side. He was wearing rubber fishing gear that kept him dry in the water. There were two trailers parked there, and two aluminum boats were pulled up on the bank.

Suddenly, two scuba divers surfaced and looked around. Holly spotted them first. "Look, I think those are the divers we saw before," she said.

When the divers realized they'd been spotted, they immediately dove below the surface.

"There's something suspicious about those guys," said Paul. "They certainly don't want to be seen. I wonder what they're up to."

The divers stayed down under and didn't resurface anywhere near the four young searchers.

"We don't have time to worry about them," said Ted, "but I agree. I think they're up to no good."

"I wonder if they had anything to do with the robbery at the camp," said Holly. "They certainly are acting in a suspicious manner, and like Paul said, they don't want to be seen. They have every right to swim or dive in this lake, so why are they hiding from us?"

"Yeah, I wonder," said Ted. "We'll find out before we leave."

"Don't you miss our dive boat?" Holly asked.

"I sure do," said Paul. "Wouldn't it be great in this lake?"

"Absolutely!" said Holly. "When we get home, we'll have to go for a run in it to Lyndaman Island. We've been so spoiled this summer. This is the first time we've had to go without all our toys. But I have to say that so far I'm enjoying this holiday. We're doing what we like to do. Search and rescue is one of our favourite things to do."

"Have you wondered what could have happened to Susannah? I thought about it till late last night," said Bonnie.

"Me too," replied Holly. "I've been thinking of all kinds of horrible things that could have happened to her. I even wondered if our elusive scuba divers might have had something to do with her disappearance."

"Me too," Bonnie exclaimed. "They're certainly acting in a very suspicious manner. Scuba divers are usually very friendly and helpful to one another, although sometimes we've found that they aren't always. But usually they're friendly. When they haven't been friendly, we've always found they were up to no good."

"That's what I was thinking" said Holly. "Oh look! I think that's one of the derelict cabins we were told about. Let's pull the canoe up on the bank and take a look."

"Okay," said Paul. "I'll turn the motor off, and we can paddle in." He lifted it out of the water so it wouldn't get caught in the weeds.

"There's a good spot," said Ted as he pointed to a small clearing under the trees. "Wow! The weeds are really thick here. I'm glad we're not swimming in this area, but it's a good spot for fishing. The fish like to hide in the weeds."

They reached the shore and pulled the canoe up the bank and under a huge pine tree. There was a faint path leading up to the cabin, but the path didn't appear to have been used recently. They followed Ted as he cleared branches and debris away from the site.

The cabin was boarded up with shutters over the windows and a padlock on the door. Slates had fallen off the roof, and the porch was rotting, pieces of which had fallen down. The steps were also rotting and were definitely unsafe. The guys poked around looking for signs of life, but it was obvious there'd been no life around the building in a very long time.

"Nothing," said Ted disappointedly. "We're wasting our time here. Let's go."

"You're right," Holly agreed. "Let's get out of here. It's pretty desolate."

They made their way back to the canoe and were soon back on the water. There was no sign of life on the lake. The fisherman was no longer there, so they decided to check another cabin out before calling it a night. About two hundred yards further on along the shoreline, they found another old cabin.

"This one seems in worse shape than the other one," said Holly. "It looks rather creepy. The bushes and trees are almost swallowing it up. I don't think there's been any life around here in decades, but let's take a look anyway."

They parked the canoe on the bank and tentatively pushed their way through the trees and bushes till they reached the cabin. It was like something from the haunted woods of a fairy tale. The girls shivered in trepidation, almost expecting something to jump out at them.

"I wonder if there are any wolves here," said Bonnie. She had never forgotten the time they were terrorized by wolves in the cave on Garibaldi Mountain when they were on the search and rescue mission to find the family that had disappeared.

"It's possible," said Ted, "but they don't usually come this close to humans. They like the higher mountainous terrain. Don't worry, Bonnie, I'll protect you." The others laughed uproariously at this comment.

Suddenly, the kids heard a squealing, mewling sound, and a rather large black cat dashed across in front of them and into the bushes. The girls screamed until they realized what it was, and then they all burst into a fit of giggles.

"Oh, that scared the life out of me," gasped Holly, "and it was only a cat. All your talk about wolves, Bonnie, has got me unhinged. Let's get out of this haunted forest before we lose it completely."

"I'm with you, Holly," said Bonnie. "Besides, it's almost nine o'clock, and we have to take the canoe back to the campground and meet up with the other searchers at the tourist booth by nine thirty."

"Right on," said Paul. "Let's go."

When they arrived at the camp, Socrates greeted them excitedly, his great tail swishing like a baton. Andy and his wife, Sheila, were pouring out cups of hot chocolate, and Sheila insisted they have a cup.

They took five minutes to drink it and fill Andy in on their exploits.

Socrates excitedly passed from one to the other to receive a hug, and Andy said he was great with the kids. They all loved him. He certainly seemed right at home. When they told Andy about checking on the two cabins, he said no one had used them in the past ten years or so, but the one by the old dance hall was sometimes rented out. It wasn't in great shape, but it was in better condition than the others.

"And some people don't really care about the condition as long as there's shelter from the weather," he said. "There's also an outhouse toilet facility for that cabin."

"We have to go," said Holly. "We have a meeting at the tourist booth at 9:30. We only have eight minutes to get there. We'll be back here shortly after that. Don't forget, we have a swimming class in the morning at ten o'clock. Please remind all the kids to be on time, because we have to leave at eleven sharp to join the search teams."

"They've been practicing most of the day," said Andy. "Some of them are better than others, but at least they're all swimming."

"Glad to hear it," said Paul. "Well, we'll see you later."

When they arrived at the tourist booth, most of the other teams were already there. Detective Brannigan and the professor were huddled in a conversation with officers Cliff and Roland. The professor called Ted and Paul over to join them, and Holly and Bonnie moved close enough to hear what they were discussing. From what they could make out, there hadn't been much progress. One team hadn't checked in yet, but they'd been in touch by radio and were on their way.

Just then, Lawrence and his team came through the trees. They'd been following the power lines running parallel to the road. The bushes were thick in this area. Further west along the road on the south side of the highway was Emerald Lake. The waters in this lake were a definite emerald green because it was thick with algae. It looked so beautiful from the highway.

It was difficult hiking through the thick foliage. The men worked to cut a path by hacking the foliage with small axes and knives. They didn't make much progress, but everyone was determined in their search for one small woman, so they pressed on.

Each team had a story to tell about their difficulties, but no one wanted to quit; however, darkness was descending, so there was no choice but to stop for the day. They all had an idea now what they would need to bring with them tomorrow in the form of equipment, and some of them took notes to remind themselves.

"We'll stay with the lake," said Paul. "Since that's where she was heading, we have a feeling we should continue there."

"I think you're right," said the professor. "Keep doing what you're doing, but be careful in the bushes. They're very thick, and I heard a grizzly bear was spotted on the south side near the road. If you see it, don't go anywhere near it, and call it in."

"Don't worry! We're not crazy enough to tackle a grizzly," said Ted.

"Oh no! First wolves, and now it's a bear," moaned Bonnie. "I've never been close to a grizzly bear. Do you think that cat today was trying to tell us something?"

"Could be," said Ted, "but whatever you do, don't pet or stroke a bear. Wolves look like dogs, but you don't pet them, and you sure don't try to pet a bear, even if you've read the story of Goldilocks."

"What have we got ourselves into?" Bonnie moaned.

"Are you allowed to carry weapons here?" Holly asked.

"Only if it's hunting season," said Ted.

"Okay, everyone!" the professor said. "Now that everybody is here and you've all had a taste of what's expected of you, we'll talk about tomorrow. If anyone has decided they don't want to do this tomorrow, just let me or Detective Brannigan know before we leave here, and we'll find someone in your place. It's not easy work, so you don't need to feel bad if you decide you can't do it. If you'd like to work in a different area, please let us know now and we'll assign you to another team."

Nobody complained, so tomorrow was a go for everyone.

"What about you, Milton?" asked Cliff. "Won't you be working?"

"I'll get my sister, Ginny, to work for me. I'm available."

"Great! You know those bushes better than I do, and you did a good job today keeping all the teams on the right trails," said Cliff.

"We'll be starting tomorrow morning at 8:00 a.m.," said the professor. "Holly's team has agreed to begin at seven, because they're teaching a swimming class from ten to eleven, and they want to get as many hours in as everyone else. We'll meet here at the tourist booth at 8:00 a.m. If you get here by 7:45, there will be doughnuts and beverages for you. If anyone needs a ride, let us know before you leave and we'll arrange one for you. Lunch will be served here at the booth at twelve noon. We're having pizza and pop delivered." A cheer went up at this announcement.

Holly raised her hand.

"Yes, Holly?" said the professor.

"Since we'll be starting at the lake at seven in the morning,we won't meet you here at eight, but we will be here for lunch."

"That sounds good, Holly," said the professor. "We'll see you at noon."

"Would all the team leaders please assemble over here," said the professor. "We'll go over your progress today and see if we can improve on it. If you have any suggestions, we'd like to hear them."

"I have a suggestion," said Milton.

"Okay Milton, let's hear it," said the detective.

"Well, I know about a small cave at Emerald Lake. I think we should take a look at it. Not too many people know about it."

"I didn't know that," said Cliff.

"Well, it's not easy to reach it, and there are a lot of wild mountain goats around that mountain. Most people are afraid the goats will attack them, so they avoid the area."

"I didn't know that either," said Cliff. "Of course, I'm not a hunter, so I don't go into the mountains unless it's necessary to follow a perpetrator."

"Me too," nodded Roland.

"There are also abandoned coal mines that have been boarded up," Milton pointed out.

"Are we going on the assumption that someone might have kidnapped Susannah? If we are, then those are viable places to hide her," said Holly. "We've been discussing Susannah's disappearance, and we were wondering if the two suspicious scuba divers might have had anything to do with it. Also, the robbery at the camp—could they be involved in that as well?"

"That's a lot of assumptions," warned the professor.

"And what about her new car?" said Milton. "Do you think they might have stolen her car?"

"Now that would be motive," said Cliff. "I'll phone the station to see if there has been any news about that little car."

He called the station and spoke to Dell, but there was no news about the car.

"We just filed the APB today, but there's been nothing reported about it," Dell told him. "It's pretty difficult to hide a red car in these small towns, especially a brand spanking new one, although it could be in a garage somewhere out of sight. We'll have to keep an eye out for strangers."

Cliff told Del to pass the word around and to tell Steve and Mort to question every stranger they saw and phone him if they saw anything that seemed even a little bit suspicious. "Susannah's been missing for three days," he reminded Dell, "and it's cold in the mountains at night."

"I hope that girl is in some kind of shelter," said Roland. "It's supposed to rain tonight, and we always get fog with the rain."

"Okay, everybody," said the professor, "let's go back to the campgrounds and get a good night's sleep tonight. Try to not be late in the morning. If you think of anything we might have missed in our plans, get here early and we can go over them before we set out."

The searchers dispersed. Holly and her team headed for the lake camp. When they arrived, Andy had his guitar out and the kids were singing campfire songs and gospel choruses. Sheila greeted them with steaming mugs of hot chocolate and insisted they have some, which they were happy to accept, but not before they each got their instruments from their saddle bags. Danny immediately ran into the hall to get the keyboard for Bonnie.

For the next thirty minutes or so, the music flowed till the parents decided it was time for the kids to go to bed. Paul reminded them that there would be a swimming class in the morning, so they'd better get lots of sleep. Holly and her friends filled in Andy and the staff on what had transpired that day, and Andy said he didn't know there was a cave at Emerald Lake.

"I can't believe I've lived here for ten years and didn't know there was a cave there," he said. "I didn't even know about the mountain goats, but then I was never a hiker, and I was so busy running this place, I didn't have time to go hiking in the wilderness."

Socrates was in doggie heaven lying at Holly's feet. His tail was swishing so hard, he could beat a rug with it.

"Were you a good boy today, Socrates?" she asked as she petted him affectionately.

"He's the best dog I've ever seen," said Andy. "The kids are crazy about him. I think I'll have to get one, but I just don't know what kind to get."

"The professor would help you with that. You want a dog that will guard the camp but also be gentle with the kids."

"Right! You're absolutely right," Andy agreed. "Help yourselves to some more hot chocolate," he urged them. "You didn't get a chance to enjoy it before, since you were busy playing and singing. I'm amazed that you know so many choruses. The kids would keep you playing and singing all night. Do you play as a group in church?"

"Yes," said Holly. "Ted's mother is a musical director. We've been in several of her musicals, and Ted has been in musicals since he was three years old. The last one we did was the story of Joseph, and we were all in it. Ted is a classically trained singer, as I'm sure you can tell by his voice."

"Yes, he is very blessed to have such talent," said Andy. "And we are very pleased that you all arrived when you did. We were blessed to share in the joy you brought with you when you filled in for the swim coach and presented us with the delightful impromptu concert. I'm not going to forget this week. It's taught me that nothing is ever as hopeless as it seems. Now if we can just find Susannah, and if she's okay, then we'll see the rainbow in the sky."

"We'll just have to pray that God is watching over Susannah," said Holly. "She must be feeling very lonely right now and wondering if anyone is looking for her."

"Yes," said Bonnie. "I keep thinking about that grizzly bear, and I'm hoping he didn't find her."

"Think positive thoughts, Bonnie," said Holly. "I think it's the two-legged variety of animal we have to worry about. Oh, oh … I just felt raindrops on my face. Let's get the tents ready for the night. I hope it doesn't rain like it did at Slocan Lake."

"Me too. I wonder what's keeping Peggy and the other kids. Did they change their minds about staying here tonight?" wondered Bonnie.

"Oh no, I should have told you. They went into town to get some supplies," Holly informed her. "I said we had enough for everybody, but she said her mom baked some special pies and other goodies for us. The others went along for the ride."

"Well, I'll never say no to pies and goodies," said Bonnie. "Let's hurry and put the tent up, and maybe we'll have time to set up the other tents before the rain begins pelting down. Won't they all be surprised when they arrive and find they won't get soaked erecting their shelter, because Andy's special angels are on the job."

Holly laughed as she told Bonnie to take the other end of the tent. They shook the heavy waterproof material until the wrinkles were all smoothed out. Bonnie took the hammer and pounded the guy wire pegs into the ground, while Holly hooked the ties onto the pegs. Then they both hoisted the tent onto the tent poles and tied them down. It was a very roomy space with a sealed waterproof floor. Within minutes, the two girls had it looking like home sweet home. "Yeah!" Holly shouted proudly with a smile of pride on her face.

Danny had thoughtfully tossed them a couple of hooded yellow sou'wester capes, so they were reasonably dry underneath. They started on Peggy and Laurie's tent, and by the time they were finished, the rain was daring them to get inside the tents and stay there. However, the other kids had not returned yet. The two girls were becoming very proficient at erecting tents by this time, and the rain urged them strongly to finish the job.

Danny and another guy named Buzz came over and helped to erect the third tent. They put it up quickly, and the girls were happy to get in out of the rain. Socrates beat them inside and picked a spot.

"Thank you, guys," said Bonnie. "I think we're in for a real storm. I'm hoping it won't be a Niagara Falls like it was at Slocan Lake."

Andy came running out with a raincoat over his head.

"Are you going to be alright there?" he asked Holly.

"Oh, we'll be fine," said Holly. "We've been in some really bad storms and managed to be comfortable enough. We've got halogen lamps and warm sleeping bags, and our tents are sealed, so we should be okay."

"Well, if you find it too much, we can set you up in the cabins, no charge. There are four empty right now. It's the end of summer, and people are getting the kids ready for school, so it's not a busy week."

"I'm sure we'll be just fine, Andy," said Holly. "But thank you for the offer. We're really quite comfortable in the tents."

Just then, Peggy's car and the bikes arrived, and the kids all piled out, the girls squealing as they stepped out into the rain. They made a beeline for the tents, shouting their thanks to Holly and Bonnie for erecting the shelters. Ted and Paul carried coolers of food, and everybody made it inside without getting too wet.

"Thanks, girls," said Paul. "We weren't looking forward to setting the tents up in the rain. You're our heroes today."

"Well, Danny and Buzz helped us, so you can thank them too."

"We'll thank them in the morning," said Ted. "I'm not moving out of here tonight. Say goodnight, Paul! See you in the morning, guys." He zipped up the tent flap.

Magen bunked with Peggy and Lorrie. Charlie and Sally had decided to stay in their parent's motorhome in town. They would see them tomorrow at lunch time. Tomorrow would be a big day. They'd covered a lot of ground in one day, and since they were starting at seven in the morning, they would need to get a good night's sleep.

Holly set up the halogen light and spread the map out on the floor.

"I'd like to check that cabin out that was all covered over with ferns and bushes," said Holly. "I keep thinking somebody must be feeding that cat, otherwise it wouldn't stick around there."

"Well, maybe there are lots of mice there. The cat didn't look like it was starving to me," Bonny mused. "But I do wonder what scared it. We'll check the cabins out tomorrow morning, and then I think we should check out the mines."

"Good idea," Holly agreed. "We'll talk to the guys about it in the morning. Okay, let's get some shut-eye. Six o'clock comes early in the a.m." They snuggled down into their sleeping bags, and Holly turned out the light. The rain was pelting down on the tents, but the trees gave then enough shelter to protect them from the wind. It wasn't long before they were in dreamland. Socrates snuggled between the two sleeping bags and was soon snoring.

The rain didn't keep them awake, but in the middle of the night, Socrates began to growl. Both girls sat up immediately. Confused with sleep, they tried to figure out what had alerted Socrates.

"What is it, Socrates?" Holly whispered. "What did you hear?" The dog kept growling.

"Maybe he wants to go out," suggested Bonnie.

Holly pulled the zipper down on the door flap, and Socrates bounded through it, barking loud enough to waken up the dead.

"There's somebody out there," said Holly. "He wouldn't do that unless he heard something."

The girls grabbed the sou'westers and pulled them on over their pyjamas. As they were pulling on their boots, Paul and Ted came out of their tent.

"What's up?" Paul shouted. "Socrates is going to waken the whole camp."

"He heard something," Holly answered as she raced past him. "He's headed down to the boat launch."

Ted and Paul followed the girls. Peggy and the other two girls poked their heads out of their tent and realized something was up. They grabbed some rain wear and their boots to join in the chase. Soon they were joined by Andy and his staff.

Socrates led them on a merry chase down to the pier, where they found him with his four legs splayed and barking up a storm. Holly and Bonny got there in time to see two heads bobbing in the water, but on realizing they'd been spotted, the rogues disappeared under the surface. Two of the canoes were loose and floating about thirty feet away from the pier. Their rope ties were trailing behind.

"They were after two more canoes," said Holly. "It's amazing they would hit the same place twice in a row. Did somebody call 911? The police might be able to catch them as they leave the lake."

"I called 911," said Andy. "Cliff and Roland are on their way. That settles it. We're getting a dog. If it hadn't been for Socrates, we'd have lost two more canoes tonight, and who knows what else."

"Good boy, Socrates," said Holly as she petted and stroked the excited dog's wet fur.

By this time, half the camp was awake, and the men had joined the group at the pier.

"What a great dog," said one of them. "I didn't hear a thing, and I'm a light sleeper."

Paul and Ted stripped down to their speedos and plunged into the cold water to secure the two canoes. They were tying them up to the slips when Cliff and Roland pulled in with their police cruiser.

"Crazy time of the night to go for a dip," said Cliff jokingly. "Are you boys okay?"

"We will be," said Ted, "when we get some clothes on. The water's really cold. The thieves got away, but you might be able to catch them if you can figure out where they're entering and leaving the water."

"We'll be checking out the abandoned cabins in the morning," said Paul, "but I don't think these guys are staying at the lake."

"What makes you say that?" Cliff asked.

"I think they have the little red car. Where could they hide it at the lake? There are only two places where they could drive the car in to park it. The rest is all brush."

"They might be holed up in one of the cabins or in a lean-to in the bushes," said Ted. "There are plenty of places where they could find shelter around the lake, but you're right about the car. It would be difficult to drive it into the brush without getting stuck. It's probably hidden somewhere else."

"Then they must have some other way to get around," said Cliff. "Probably mountain bikes. They could ride through the bush on them. But how would they move the canoes?"

"Don't worry," said Ted. "We'll find them, but not tonight. They're long gone. I'm going back to bed. Don't forget we have to get up at 6:00

a.m. which is only three hours from now. You need to get chains with padlocks for the canoes, Andy."

"You're right, but Socrates is a good guard dog," said Andy. "He'll let us know if those rascals come back again. I'm for going to bed too. Let's call it a night. Thanks for coming so quickly, Cliff."

"We'll be on shift till 7:00 a.m., but I'll be here at 10:00 a.m. for the swimming class. I'll see you all in a few hours."

Everybody headed for their beds. Holly and Bonnie hugged Socrates and gave him lots of love and petting for being such a brave dog. He lapped it up like the champion he was and then found his spot between the two sleeping bags and settled down for the rest of the night.

The thieves didn't come back, and the rain eased off before morning, so when the sun came up, everything was fresh, clean, and green.

Tumbledown Cabins

CHAPTER 7

HOLLY'S WATCH ALARM VIBRATED AT 6:00 A.M., AND SHE NUDGED BONNIE awake. She yawned and stretched, willing her body to climb out of bed and greet the new day. Bonnie gave a few little squeaks to let her know she was awake. It took a few more minutes before they rolled out of the sleeping bags, and with a moan and a groan or two, they started to pull on their jeans and the rest of their clothes.

Holly began to root through the cooler, and soon had a decent breakfast laid out. By then the two guys were up and dressed and had joined them. There was always food wherever they went, because Holly never went anywhere without her duffle bag. They also had the cooler that Peggy and Lorrie's mom had sent with them the previous evening.

Peggy and Lorrie didn't have to get up until 7:00 a.m., because they were assigned to another team that didn't start until 8:00 a.m. Holly let them sleep and would give them a wake-up call as her group was leaving the camp after breakfast to check out the abandoned cabins around the lake. Andy had told them they could leave their food in the kitchen cooler, so it wouldn't go bad in the heat.

"It's a beautiful day," said Holly. "If we just coast along the shoreline, there should be plenty of little inlets that we can pull into. Most of the cabins are close to the water, so we should be able to find old trails leading to them."

"We'll take some tools to help us blaze a trail," said Ted.

When they finished breakfast, they packed what they needed into the largest canoe and then stopped at the girl's tent to waken them for the day's adventures.

"Wow! I can't believe it's morning already," said Lorrie. Magen blinked as she wiped the sleep from her eyes.

"The food is in our tent," said Holly. "Don't forget to put the cooler and duffle bag into the kitchen cooler before you go."

"Don't worry," said Peggy. "We'll take care of it."

"We'll see you at noon," said Holly. "Let's hope we have more success today."

They said their goodbyes and were off. Paul started the motor and took command of the tiller. The lake was calm, and the canoe slipped through the water like an eel.

"This is a great time of the day to be on the water," said Ted.

"Yes, if only we could find Susannah," added Bonnie. "I hope she had shelter last night from the rain."

"I keep praying she's still alive," said Holly.

"We're going to assume that she is," Ted said firmly. "Think of all the situations we've been in before when we didn't expect to find the victims alive, but we did. They weren't always in the best shape, but they were alive, and where there is life, there's hope. We'll find her."

"How did you get to be so wise?" teased Bonnie.

"We just have to believe," he said. "And Susannah has to believe that someone is out there looking for her. Can you imagine how she feels? We've seen some of the places the perpetrators have stashed their hostage victims before. Remember Lyndaman Island and the tunnels, and Garibaldi Mountain and the mine and root cellar? I just hope she's being fed and that they aren't abusing her."

"You're right. We have to have faith that she's not being mistreated," said Holly. "It would make us crazy to think otherwise, so let's keep to the plan and pray that God will lead us to her like He did on the other missions. Let's pull in to that little inlet up ahead. I think I see a cabin through the trees."

Paul steered the canoe into the small cleft in the rocks. There was a little beach inlet with no sand, but it was covered in tiny, smooth pebbled rocks and surrounded by thick bushes. They hopped out of the canoe, pulled it up the bank, and hid it in the bushes. Ted immediately pushed his way through the dense brush, swinging a small ax to cut a trail.

"There's a cabin about two hundred feet in," he said. "I can see the roof through the trees. It doesn't look like anyone's been in here in a very long time."

The others picked their way over the broken branches and did their best to follow their tracking leader. Ted had done this many times before and was an expert at reading the signs.

"I hope there aren't any bears or wolves," said Bonnie.

"There've been lots of animals through here," said Ted. "I think they use this area to make their way to the lake for drinking water. I can see some faint trails and some spoor from all different sizes of animals."

"What kinds of animals?" Bonnie asked in a shaky voice.

"I'm not sure," said Ted, "but I'm sure there are probably bears, moose, and deer. I don't think mountain goats would come down here. They like to stay in the mountains. I don't know the area, so I'm not familiar with the kinds of animals that live here. Don't worry, Bonnie, the animals usually don't come near you unless you bother them."

"I hope they know that rule," said Bonnie, "because I definitely won't be bothering them."

They could see the cabin through the trees now. The bushes and trees were dense except at the front door, which was padlocked. They assumed nobody was home, but also remembered the time when a family was locked in the root cellar of an abandoned cabin at Garibaldi Mountain. There was a padlock on that door too, so they knew they should at least check it out. Paul picked his way over tangled branches to scout around the side of the building. The girls tried to see through the dirty windows but could see nothing. Paul was back in a couple of minutes.

"There's a padlock on the back door as well," he said. "The back steps are in bad shape. They're pretty busted up."

"So is the rest of the cabin," announced Ted.

"Have you guys noticed this?" asked Holly.

"Noticed what?" said Ted.

"The padlocks," she pointed. "This one is like brand new. What about the back door?" she asked Paul.

"Now that you mention it," he said, "that padlock was like new too."

"Looking at the condition of the rest of this place," said Holly, "and taking into consideration the recent weather conditions, the padlocks should be old and rusted. Somebody has been out here recently. They've changed the locks, and I have to wonder why."

"Yeah, this old relic should be torn down before it falls down," said Ted. "Let's check the windows. Maybe we can open one. I wonder if something is being hidden here."

"Like what?" Bonnie asked.

"Maybe drugs, or stolen goods, or people," said Holly. "It just seems suspicious that someone would put new padlocks on an old falling down shack that you could pull apart with your bare hands. What would be valuable enough to require two new locks? Andy said all these old cabins were uninhabitable and should be torn down. He said there was no one living in them. The other abandoned cabins that we entered were wide open."

"It's one thing to walk into an abandoned cabin that's wide open," said Paul, "but we might be in trouble if we enter a shack that's been locked down regardless of its condition."

"You're right," said Holly. "Why don't we wait till we talk to Officer Cliff. We'll be seeing him in a couple of hours. We can go on to the next cabin in the meantime."

"I agree," said Ted. "We want to be strictly legal and not open ourselves up to a break and enter charge."

They headed back down to the lake and retrieved their canoe. Ted scanned the area and noticed there was no one else on the lake—no fishermen, no scuba divers, and no small boats or canoes. Usually there were at least a couple of fishermen either out in boats or fly fishing from shore. It was too early for the small kids to be in the water.

There was another tiny inlet just a little farther on, so Paul eased the canoe up to the bank. Ted pulled it in beside a large rock, and the girls climbed out without getting their feet wet. They found a great clump of bushes and hid the canoe behind them, just in case the rogue scuba divers happened to be in the area.

"This shack is in even worse shape than the others," said Ted. "The lean-to on the side is caved in and falling down, and the front door has been bashed in."

"Well, in the condition it's in, we shouldn't get into trouble if we go inside," said Holly. "It's very unlikely it holds anything of interest."

"Wait till Ted and I check it out in case there are animals in there," said Paul. "When it's wide open like this, you never know what you're going to find."

"I'm with you there," said Bonnie. "I don't want another scare like the army of bats that wanted to make a nest in my hair, or the wolves that threatened us at Garibaldi Mountain."

Holly chuckled and grinned at her best friend's trepidation where some animals were concerned.

"It's alright for you, Holly ... you aren't scared of anything, but someday you'll meet something that scares you, and your legs will turn to rubber like mine, and you won't be able to run."

"I'm sorry, Bonnie. You're right, but it's not true that I don't get scared. I get scared just like you. We're just afraid of different things, and I don't like the guys to think we're scared because we're girls, so I bite my tongue and pretend I'm as tough as they are. Since we sometimes work with Search and Rescue, I realize we have to be strong both physically and mentally. It doesn't mean I'm not afraid sometimes, but I always tell myself it'll turn out okay."

The guys seemed to be taking a long time to check out the cabin, and the girls were beginning to wonder what they were doing, when suddenly they were assailed with frightening yips and hollers from inside the cabin. The guys came crashing through the broken door, with Ted pointing a long stick ahead of him.

"Out of the way," he shouted as he ran past the girls towards a large clump of bushes. A large snake was curled around the stick, its tail dangling. As the guys rushed by, the girls ran screaming in the opposite direction, and Ted aimed the stick like a javelin as far as he could into the dense forest greenery.

"Ugh, gross." Holly was almost gagging. "I hate snakes," she shouted as she shivered and shook. "You have no idea how I feel around snakes, Bonnie." Her face had drained of all colour, and she appeared as if she might faint.

"Now you know how I feel," said Bonnie. "I don't think I'm as afraid of snakes as you are; I just don't like them. My brother used to have one as a pet. I never made a friend of it, but I did threaten him that if he ever let it loose in my room, he would sleep in the barn with his snake."

"I don't like snakes either," said Ted. "I always think of them as serpents. We had one in one of Mom's musicals once. It freaked most of the cast out, but Mom used to pet it, and that freaked me out."

"I wouldn't have been in that musical for all the money in the world," said Holly. "If it came near me on stage, they would have had to use smelling salts on me, because I would faint dead away if it came within ten feet of me."

"Well, there was nothing inside the cabin except for an old broken down iron bedstead and a pile of garbage in one corner."

"Then what took you so long?" asked Holly.

"We were poking through the garbage with sticks when the snake crawled out of one particularly nasty smelling pile and latched on to the stick," said Ted. "I didn't have any choice but to get rid of it. Do you still want to go in? There's nothing else in there."

"No, I don't think so. The snake took all the fun out of it for me. We'll take your word for it that there's nothing there," said Holly.

"Okay then, let's move on," said Paul. "There's another cabin seven hundred feet further on." He was checking the map as Ted slid the canoe down the bank. The girls were already climbing in.

"I want to get out of here in case that snake comes looking for us," said Holly.

"We have time for one more cabin," said Ted. "Then we have to get back to camp for the swimming lessons."

"Yes, I'm looking forward to teaching Cliff," said Paul. "I have to admire him for wanting to learn with a class of young kids. Sam too. He did very well, and Willie was so excited for his dad."

The weather was holding out, and the canoe and little 4 HP motor putted along at a nice easy pace. The morning had slipped away so quickly. Where did the time go? It was now 9:15 a.m. They would have to hurry if they were going to get back to the camp by 10:00 a.m.

Paul steered the canoe into the bank. There wasn't an inlet here, but at one time there had been a pier. The pier walkway was missing struts and poles and obviously hadn't been used in decades. An old boat house was partially standing, but not usable, and considering the condition of the structure, it was odd that there was a padlock on the door. Twenty feet or so behind it stood another dilapidated cabin.

It was in better shape than the others, but not fit for anyone to live in, not even as a summer cottage. The door was closed, but it wasn't locked. Holly and Bonnie were quite happy when Paul and Ted went in to check the place out. It took only a few minutes to look into the closets and cupboards to decide the place was safe for the girls to enter.

"It's all clear," said Ted. "You can come in now. There are no signs of snakes or bogey men, but it appears that someone has been using the building for a shelter."

"Why do you say that?" Holly asked.

"There are pizza cartons and fast food paper cups and plates that don't look like they've been here very long."

"And somebody has swept the floor with that old broom," said Paul. "There are two sleeping bags, and they seem pretty clean, and there's a box of items over here that includes canned meat and various food supplies."

"Maybe we shouldn't be in here," said Holly. "But Andy said that only one of the cabins was inhabitable, and that's the one beside the old dance hall."

"Let's get out of here," said Paul. "We can come back after class. I'd like to check out that old boathouse, but it's so dilapidated I want to be wearing my scuba gear when I do. It's quite deep under there, and it might collapse and pin us down if we walk inside, so for protection and just to be on the safe side, I'll wear my gear and air tank. Ted will come with me for buddy protection. You two can wait until we check it out. We'll enter it from the water by swimming underneath. That way we won't be walking on rotten boards."

"That's a good idea," said Holly. "Well, we've only got twenty minutes to get back to the camp. The little motor isn't equipped for speed, so let's go!"

They pulled into the slip at the camp with five minutes to spare. The kids were all ready and waiting, excitement written all over their faces. Sam and Cliff were standing beside a very excited Willie. The other coaches were all there and ready to begin.

"You made it," Cliff greeted them. "How did the search go this morning?" he asked.

"We have lots to tell you," said Ted, "but we'll wait until after the lesson. The kids are excited to get going, so we won't keep them waiting. Okay, kids," he shouted over the chatter, "I want you all to gather around. We're going to see how well you've practiced first, and then we're going to do some more exercises for your next lesson. Everybody into the water."

"I'll take Officer Cliff with my group this morning," said Paul. "Cliff is starting from scratch, so he'll need some extra help to catch up. The rest of you join the coaches you had yesterday, and stay with them."

There was a mad scramble while the children formed their prearranged groups from the previous day's class. It was like magic the way Paul clapped his hands and they came to attention at once.

"When your teacher says "go," reach out with your arms and sweep them all the way around as wide as you can, breathing in and out, and kick. Pretend that you're a canoe and your arms and hands are the oars. Keep your fingers tightly together, and pretend your hands are the paddles on the end of the oars. When you sweep your arms in a half circle, you're pushing the water back. If you do that, you'll move forward. Now let's see what you remember from yesterday and apply this new lesson. Okay, coaches, go for it."

The coaches took over, and on the command to go, twenty children, plus Sam, became serious about their breathing, sweeping, and kicking and tried to outdo each other in the water. It was a sight to behold. The coaches helped the littlest ones who were slower at picking up the basic principles of the exercise.

Paul had asked Cliff to wait till he got the others in his group swimming, and then he began to give him tips on how to become a strong swimmer. If he was to use what he learned to someday be strong enough to help another adult who might be drowning, he would need to work twice as hard as the children, but he would first of all have to get the basics in the same way the children were learning them. But he would have a higher goal in mind.

They went through the exercises, the breathing, sweeping the arms in a half circle, and the kicking, and then Paul shouted, "Go." Cliff did a belly flop into the water, which surprised Paul, and then applied the principles that Paul had just gone over with him.

"Don't forget to breathe, Cliff," Paul coached him. "And don't worry, I won't let you drown. You're doing great. Just count as you reach out. One … two, one … two. That's it, now slow down and count slowly. Okay, you can stand up now."

Cliff was grinning. "I can't believe I did that," he said. "No wonder I couldn't swim. Breathing right and timing makes all the difference, doesn't it?"

"That's right," said Paul. "Practicing the breathing and exercises you were watching yesterday helped you on your very first try. But don't forget, you're wearing a life jacket. Now we're going to try what you just did without a life jacket."

"And here I thought I'd done a great job. I'm not sure if I can," he said nervously.

"Of course you can," said Paul. "I guarantee that if you do just what you did with the jacket on, you'll be swimming without it."

"Do you really think so?" He sounded just like Sam.

"I told you I would guarantee it. Look at Sam. He wouldn't get in the water in a life vest before I showed him how. He couldn't even dog paddle like you, and look at him now."

Sam was doing a terrific breast stroke, and he didn't even stop to take a break. He was so elated that he sounded like his son, Willie.

Father and son were shouting at each other, and Willie was challenging him to a race against him and Barney.

"Okay, I'll take it off," said Cliff. He took off the vest and handed it to Paul. "At least I'm only in less than four feet of water, so here goes."

He took several deep breaths, and then Paul shouted, "Go." Cliff did the same belly flop as before, and then took off just like Sam. "One ... two, one ... two," Paul counted. He was delighted when Cliff reached out in a wide arc as graceful as a bird. No more dog paddling for this guy. He kept on swimming for at least forty feet, and when he stopped and had his feet on the bottom, he was grinning from ear to ear.

Paul called all the kids and their coaches to join him on the bank, and when they were assembled, he praised them for the progress they'd made in such a short time.

"I'm really proud of all of you," he said. "You've come a long way in a few days, so now you're going to learn the Australian crawl. You've learned the basics, and now you know if you breathe properly, you won't sink. Close your fingers together and make a paddle, or an oar, with your hands. Now reach straight out with your right hand. Pretend you're pulling it under and back through the water just like an oar. As you're reaching back, reach straight out with your left hand, pretend it's an oar, and start pulling it down and back through the water. Continue with the right arm, and then the left."

They did the exercise until they all got the rhythm of alternating the arms.

"That's very good," said Paul. "Now instead of kicking, keep your legs together and use your feet like the tail of a fish by flicking them up and down like this." He demonstrated as he spoke. "Flick them up and down, one foot at a time, and remember to breathe in as you reach out with your arm, and breathe out as you reach back. Never stop breathing."

There was a lot of huffing and puffing as the kids tried to coordinate the exercise and breathing.

"That's a lot for you to remember, but if you practice, you'll find that you'll soon do it all automatically just like you did on the breast stroke. Practice on your bed lying on your stomach until you can do it without thinking. Okay, back in the water to try it."

Paul looked at his waterproof watch. "We still have ten minutes, and then you can practice on your own in the shallow water. Always make sure there are adults around when you're in the water, just in case you get into trouble."

Sam was floundering a bit at first and then seemed to get in the rhythm of it when he remembered to breathe properly. Cliff started out with a comical mixture of elongated dog paddle and breast stroke until his brain kicked in and he remembered to breathe. Soon he was able to reach out one arm at a time and started to feel the rhythm.

The coaches were busy. This new crawl was not easy. Some of the kids were kicking like they were doing the breast stroke, and some weren't using their feet at all, but they were doing their best to follow Paul's instructions. They were all remembering to breathe, mainly because their coaches were counting it out for them.

When their time was up, Paul called the kids together on the bank. They were pretty elated that they had come so far, and all their coaches were proud of their progress.

"Alright, kids," said Paul. "You've all done a great job so far. I can see some future champions here. All you need is practice, so every day that you're here at this beautiful lake, practice, practice, practice."

"I'm going to be a champion like you, Paul," said Willie. "I'll practice every day, even when I go home. There's a pool close to my house, and I'm going to make sure Dad goes too."

"That's great, Willie," said Paul.

The other kids all made promises that they would do the same.

"I'm so glad we did this," said Holly as she looked at all the shining faces.

"Me too," said Bonnie.

"I've lived here all my life," said Peggy, "and I never thought about coming out here and teaching kids to swim. From now on, Lorrie and I will make the offer now that Andy knows us."

"Yes, Andy shouldn't have to send out of town for a swim coach," said Lorrie.

"That's super," said Holly. "In the meantime, we have to find out what happened to Susannah, so we'd better get back on the job. We still have some time left before lunch."

Cliff phoned the police station to see if there was any news, and he seemed very excited as he got off his phone.

"Roland tells me that the little red car has been spotted in Frank. He's headed out that way, so I have to go. Thanks, Paul. I never thought I'd be able to swim, but I can see all I need is practice. I'll be here tomorrow. See you at ten."

"Maybe we'll see you in Frank," said Holly. "We wanted to see Turtle Mountain anyway, and the Frank Slide. We also want to see old Chief George, but I think we'll wait until after lunch. It's 11:15 now, and we want to take another look at a cabin we were at this morning. After that, we'll meet at the tourist booth for lunch. It's been a long time since breakfast."

"You're right," said Cliff. "Okay, we'll catch up with you later." With that, he was off.

Holly and her team grabbed their air tanks and headed for the canoes. The other coaches left to join their teams to try to get some search time in before lunch. Paul started up the little motor and took up the tiller, and they were on their way. They made it to the cabin in about ten minutes.

There was no one around when they pulled the canoe up the bank. Paul and Ted put on their air tanks and helmets and immediately slipped into the water. They swam around to the boat exit, and when they entered the ramshackle boathouse, they were amazed to discover it wasn't empty.

There were two canoes tied up to the posts. They were covered with tarps, and when they pulled the tarps back, they discovered the stolen bikes, generators, paddles, small boat motors, and several other items that the guys were sure were also stolen.

"Well," said Ted, "looks like we've found the stolen loot. Let's vamoose before we're spotted. We'll tell Cliff and let him deal with it."

"I agree," said Paul. "Let's tell the girls and head for lunch. I can smell that pizza from here."

"You're on," Ted said. "Now we have to find out what happened to Susanna. Do you think Cliff and Roland will find the car? It could be hidden in the hills around Turtle Mountain. I wonder what the terrain is like there. I hope our bikes will handle the trails."

When they told Holly and Bonnie what they'd found, the two girls were ecstatic and agreed they should get out of there as quickly as possible and inform the police. Ted called the police station on his cell, and Del said she would inform Officers Cliff and Roland immediately, and they would look into it as soon as possible.

Cliff and Roland were already in the town of Frank, but they hadn't seen the car. Their informant said there were two men in the vehicle, and it took off in a cloud of dust while he was talking to Steve on his cell. But he managed to get the license plate number, and Steve left for Frank immediately.

By the time they made it back to camp and informed Andy about their discovery, it was time for lunch, so they headed as quickly as possible to the tourist booth. The other searchers were already there, and the pizza had arrived.

"Oh, can you smell that?" said Paul, sniffing the air. "That is pure heaven. I don't know about you, but I'm starving. This has been a long morning." Everybody was already eating. "I hope they left us something," he said.

"Oh, don't you worry," said Milton. "There's enough here to feed an army. How did things go for you? We found nothing."

"Well, we found something alright," said Holly. "We didn't find Susannah, but we did find the loot."

"You did?" There was a collective shout from the other searchers. "The canoes too?" Milton asked.

"Yes, the canoes too," said Paul.

"Wow! Super cool," yelled Peggy. "But no clues about Susannah?"

"No, nothing yet," said Paul. "I think they've taken her somewhere else. Since the car was spotted in Frank, maybe that's where we should be looking."

"Yes," said Holly. "We've decided to take a look in Frank and the mines surrounding the town. That's where we're going after lunch."

"I think that's a good idea," said the professor, "but keep in touch with either Detective Brannigan or me, or call 911 for the police on your cell if you run into trouble. We'll keep on searching around the lake and in the bush. She could be anywhere, so we need to cover as much of this area as we can. And we need to get into these fellows' heads and think like them."

"Hmm … that could be messy. Where do you think they'd stash a young woman?" said Paul. "We have to assume she's alive, at least until we find out differently. And we need to find out where they bought the fast food that came in the cartons we found at the cabin. Maybe they're buying food for her. Let's hope they are. If we can locate the venue, we could place a lookout in the vicinity to watch out for the little red car."

"If they show up, the lookout could call us or the police if he believes he's found the culprits," said Detective Brannigan. "He could follow at a distance, keeping us informed, so we'll know at all times where he is. We don't want anyone getting lost or in trouble. Like Paul says, we must assume she's alive. Let's hope we're not looking for a body."

"One thing I noticed," said Holly, "was that there was no advertising on the cartons. That's unusual."

"Well, there aren't many fast food venues in the Pass," said Peggy, "so it shouldn't be too difficult to discover which one uses those containers."

"We did keep a bag of the containers," said Holly. "There were pizza cartons and what looked like Chinese food containers. We were careful about handling them in case there were fingerprints on them."

"Good girl," said her father. "I can see I taught you well. I doubt the scoundrels were wearing gloves while they were eating, so there will definitely be fingerprints."

"We also kept some of the bottles and cans, in case the police wanted to check for DNA."

"Even better," the detective grinned broadly. "I can certainly envision the sign 'Brannigan and Brannigan, Attorneys at Law and Investigation' in our future."

Holly grinned back at him. "Thank you, Daddy, but you'll also have to find room on that sign for Paul's name too. We both plan to be lawyers."

"Good for you, Paul. When the time comes, we'll talk. And what about you, Ted?" the detective asked. "Have you decided what your future will hold?"

"I'm going in for architecture," Ted answered. "Mr. Fields said he would mentor me and bring me into his firm when I graduate."

"That's wonderful!" the detective said. "And what about you, Bonnie? What are you going to do?"

"I don't know yet," she said. "I thought I might like to get into fashion."

"That's good," said Holly. "I'll need you to show me how to dress like a lawyer."

"Well, it's good to have a dream," said the professor. "Far too many young people don't have a clue what the future holds for them, and they find themselves in their thirties without a career and no plans for the future."

The pizza was delicious, and they were almost finished eating when Officers Cliff and Roland pulled into the lot. They hurried over to the table. Roland was sniffing the air like a bloodhound.

"Oh, it smells so good," he said. "I hope you left us some."

"There's lots here," said Holly. "Help yourself. As a matter of fact, I was wondering if you know which restaurant delivers pizza and hamburgers in plain cartons with no advertising on them."

"Well, I can see that this pizza came from, Lorenzo's," said Cliff, and Roland nodded in agreement as he stuffed his mouth full of the house special. "He has the best pizza in town, but he does advertise. Didn't you like it?"

"Oh, of course. It was delicious!" she replied. She told them about the cartons and cans and bottles they'd found in the cabin and how they'd bagged them for fingerprinting. The two policemen were impressed, but when she told them about the discovery of the canoes in the boathouse and the stolen items stowed under the tarps, they were over the moon.

"This is great," said Cliff. "Del just told us that you'd found some clues in a cabin, but this is terrific. I'll get Steve and some crime tech guys on it right away. I just wish we could find that young lady. We thought when we were told the car was seen in Frank that we'd be able to just go and pick them up. Our informant said there were two men in the car, but at least he got the plate number, so we know it's the right car. We'll get someone looking for the restaurant that uses plain cartons right away."

"Well, we're going into Frank to see old Chief George," said Holly. "He's supposed to know more about the history of the mines and the Slide than anybody in the area. We want to check out the mines and see if any of them appear to have been broken into. Since the car has been seen there, we thought it was possible they might have moved her and hidden her in one of the mines."

"That's entirely possible," said Cliff. "It's actually very good thinking. If your team is going into Frank, please keep in touch with us. You have your cells, and Paul has a radio for the hills just in case you can't get a signal with your cells. Call us if you see anything suspicious, but do not, under any circumstances, tackle these guys on your own. They may be armed. That's what we're here for. Roland and I are going to check out Alice Lake; there are usually a dozen tents or trailers out there. Then we'll head back to the town of Frank. You have my cell phone number. Don't hesitate to call for any reason."

"I think we'd like to take Peggy and Lorrie with us," said Holly. "Sally, Charlie, and Magen haven't been trained in search and rescue, so we'll leave them with the professor. My team has been trained to handle most situations on search and rescue missions. Peggy and Lorrie know these little towns in the Pass, so they'll be a terrific help to us."

"That's a very good idea," Cliff told them. "Let us know if you see anything suspicious, no matter how small. We'll be no more than ten or fifteen minutes away from you at any time. These little towns are no more than five or ten miles apart."

Holly approached Peggy and Lorrie and asked them to accompany her team. They were really excited to join the number one team. She explained that their familiarity with the Pass would ensure that the team wouldn't get lost, and they would be a big asset in locating the mines.

The Frank Slide

PEGGY AND LORRIE RODE ON THE BACKS OF HOLLY AND BONNIE'S BIKES, AND it seemed to take no time at all to reach the town of Frank. They gazed in awe at the destruction that had been caused by the hundreds of thousands of tons of rock that had wiped out three quarters of the town in 1903, over a hundred years ago. The very thought that all but one tiny baby in that part of town died in their sleep made the hair stand up on the back of the young explorers' necks.

A large plaque to explain the tragic history stood at the side of the road. This was the mountain that the Blackfoot called the Mountain That Moves. Some called it, The Mountain that Walks. They had warned the town's villagers that the mountain would come down, but no one paid any attention to their warnings. Even the birds and other animals had all migrated to other parts of the Pass—a good omen to anyone who was living in the vicinity that they'd better move.

But as usually happens when people have been issued warnings, the villagers ignored them. A small community at the north end of the town escaped the devastation. Two men from that part of town climbed over the rocks and ran down the railway tracks to attempt to stop a passenger train named the Spokane Flyer. One of the men had to stop part way because of exhaustion, and if not for the other man, there would have been another terrible tragedy. The aboriginals have since warned the villagers that the mountain will come down again on the other side of the town, and people are still living there playing Russian roulette with their lives.

The young explorers stood reading and gasping in silence. When they finally found their voices, they all began talking at once. They were visibly shaken. They all said, "Wow" simultaneously.

"Wow," Holly exclaimed. "It's a cemetery. I feel like the spirits of the dead are all around me."

"Me too," said Bonnie. "I feel like I'm standing on holy ground. You know how you feel when you walk through a cemetery."

"Well, in a way, it is," said Ted. "Hopefully they didn't wake up. I think being buried alive would be the worst thing that could happen to anyone."

"I agree," said Paul.

"You know, it doesn't matter how often I see this," said Peggy, "I still get shaken up like it was the first time, and I've lived here all my life."

"Me too," said Lorrie. "That's the Interpretive Centre up there. Do you want to go up and take a look out over the Slide?"

"Yes, I do," said Holly. "I want to speak to the man who spoke to Susannah when she was here."

"Good idea," said Paul. "Maybe he noticed if someone was hanging around who might have looked suspicious."

"Okay," said Holly. "We might get more information if it's a girl asking questions about another girl, so please let me talk to him."

"You're right," said Ted. "He might get suspicious if a guy asks questions about a young girl who's disappeared. I think you should question him."

The others agreed, so they headed up to the very impressive building that overlooked the Slide. They could see the wrap-around deck that jutted out over the rocks.

When the young explorers entered the building, they didn't see anyone around, so they headed for the double doors leading to the deck. When they stepped outside, they were again awestruck with horror at the sight that met their eyes. Seeing the destruction from this height was even worse than what they'd seen below. It was so indescribably horrendous, it was as though it had just happened and had a paralytic effect on their limbs.

They couldn't move. Their minds were stuck way back in 1903. It was as though they were viewing the end of the world from a great height. The span of the gigantic rocks of the fallen mountain seemed to go on forever. They stood there like they were in a trance, not saying a word, until the double doors opened and a man stepped through.

"Hi there," he said. "I didn't see you come in. I was in the storeroom sorting supplies. Sorry I missed you. My name is Alex Tyler. Welcome to the Interpretive Centre. Where are you folks from?"

Paul was the first to find his voice. "We're from Vancouver area, sir, except for Peggy and Lorrie here. They live in Blairmore."

"So you're here visiting, are you? Is this the first time you've seen the Slide?"

"Yes, sir," said Paul. "I've never seen anything like this before. We've had avalanches in B.C., but I've never seen anything that equals this. It's worse than an earthquake."

"Yes, it wiped out three quarters of the town," said Mr. Tyler. "Is there anything I can help you with? We have maps and books on the history of the Slide."

Holly finally found her voice. "Yes, Mr. Tyler, we're interested in the history of the Slide and the mines in the area."

"Well, come inside and sign the guest book, and I'll provide you with information about the hills and mines. There's really good fishing here as well. If you tell me where you'd like to go, I can give you directions. Follow me," he said as he ushered them into the centre.

"Mister Tyler, do you mind if I ask you some questions about a young lady who was here on Sunday?" asked Holly.

Mr. Tyler looked at her with a wrinkled brow. "What kind of questions?" he asked.

"Well, we're staying at the Crowsnest Lake camp, and the young lady in question was supposed to arrive there on Sunday to teach the little kids how to swim, but she never arrived. We're part of the search and rescue team that is trying to find her."

"Yes, I heard about that. She was here around closing time and was excited about teaching the kids. Les talked to her, and he was admiring her new car. He said she was a nice girl. The police asked us about her, but we couldn't help them much."

"Did you see anyone hanging around her who seemed suspicious?" she asked. "Maybe someone who might have been paying an undue amount of attention to her?"

"There were only two other young fellows here at the time. Les was the one who served her, but now that you mention it, those guys seemed to be really interested in her. But then again, she was a very beautiful girl, so what young fellow wouldn't be interested?"

"Of course," said Holly. "Could you describe them for us?"

"Well, I did get a good look at them, since they were the only other customers in the store. They didn't buy anything, but I felt that I had to watch them as they were picking things up that I could tell they had no intention of buying. They were more interested in the girl. Let me think. One of them had red hair and was wearing a black jacket with a skull and crossbones on the back, and the other one had long, scruffy, black hair, and he was wearing a tan coloured suede jacket. They were both wearing jeans with holes in the knees."

"Thank you, Mr. Tyler. If you think of anything else, please call the police and ask for Officer Cliff."

"Yes, I know Cliff. He was here yesterday. I hope you find her."

"We'd like to know about the mines and all about the disaster with the slide. We're going to see Chief George, as we've been told he's an expert on the mines."

"That's a good idea. I hope you have plenty of time, because old Chief likes nothing better than to talk about the mines and the slide. He'll talk your ears off. His father was in the mine when the mountain came down, so he knows more about it than anyone else around here. He's almost as old as the mountain itself."

"Wow! Did his father get out?" Ted asked.

"He did, but he'll tell you all about it, and make you some tea while he's at it ... his own brew."

"I'm looking forward to that," said Holly.

They looked around the Centre and were amazed at the artifacts displayed. The rocks, stones, coal, and gemstones that represented the Crowsnest Pass landscape were showcased in glass-enclosed display showcases. Turtle Mountain was represented in another glass showcase displaying limestone and coal. One room was a museum of ancient artifacts from the mines, with workable equipment and sepia coloured pictures taken a hundred years ago with ancient photographic equipment.

The kids bought a few books on the Frank Slide's history and on the mines that had operated in the Pass but were no longer in operation. The history was impressive, and they had only just begun. They said goodbye to Alex Tyler and thanked him for all the information, promising to let him know if they found Susanna.

They followed the little map that Holly had drawn to guide them to old Chief George's cabin and found themselves on a very rough, uneven trail. It wound around the mountain, and they were thankful they had the bikes. A car would have a problem on this terrain.

Old Chief George

CHAPTER 9

THANKFULLY, AS THEY MADE THE TURN, THEY SAW THE LITTLE LOG CABIN THROUGH the trees. It was set back in the middle of a grove of fir trees. Wild flowers grew all around it, and the occupant was sitting on a rocking chair on the porch, smoking a pipe. He was as old as the hills surrounding him, and he stood up with great difficulty as the kids climbed off the bikes. He waited patiently till they approached and stood in front of him.

Paul offered his hand in greeting. "Hi, I'm assuming you're Chief George. My name is Paul Castles, and these are my friends, Holly Brannigan, Bonnie Tilson, Ted Lumley, and Peggy and Lorrie Clayborn."

"Yes, I'm old Chief George. Nice to meet you," said the chief as he shook their hands. "Welcome to Turtle Mountain. What can I do for you? Are you lost?"

"No, Chief," said Paul. "We're not lost. We came to see you. Could we talk to you about the slide and the mines? We've been told you know more about their history than anyone here in the Pass."

The old chief coughed and chuckled as he studied the young folks. "I 'spect the folks are right about that. Come on in and sit down, and I'll make some tea. I don't get company very often, 'specially young folks, but I'm real partial to a bit of confab now and then. It gets mighty lonesome out here, 'cept when my grandkids come to see me."

They followed him into the cabin and were surprised to find it quite cozy. There were two lounge chairs and a leather sofa that looked quite comfortable. The chief pulled out two extra chairs from the table.

"Okay, sit and make yourselves comfortable while I put the kettle on." He went over to the sink, and they were surprised when he turned on the tap and ran the cold water to fill the kettle.

"I wouldn't have expected to see running water out here in the hills," said Holly. "How did you manage to get plumbing so far from town?"

"My grandson, Dusty, is a plumber. When he got his papers, the first thing he did was put the plumbing in here for me. Before that, they had to haul the water out here in big water tanks. Dusty said he didn't want to do that anymore, and that was why he studied to be a plumber."

While he was talking, the old chief plugged in the kettle and put several spoonsful of tea in a stoneware teapot. "Got the 'lectricity the same way. My other grandson, Jimmy, took up 'lectrical work, and before I knew what was happening, he'd set up a windmill behind the cabin to generate 'lectricity.

"He tried to get them to bring it in from the town, but the town folks said it would be too expensive. But he fixed it anyways, so I don't git a 'lectric bill or a water bill. I've got it real good out here."

"I'm glad your grandchildren are so good to you," said Holly.

"Yup, I'm a lucky man."

The old man was quite spry on his feet for someone so ancient.

"It's very kind of you to make us tea," continued Holly. "We don't mean to impose. We just want to ask you a few questions."

"Well, we can't talk without a cup of tea. In the old days, they used to pass around the peace pipe, but I like to make tea. It's my own brew. I gather the wild berries and plants and dry them out. Everybody likes my tea. People from town drop in every now and then just to have a cup."

"I'm looking forward to it," said Bonnie, who had been really quiet up until that point.

"Me too," chorused the others.

"Yup, I still do my own gathering of wild plants," the old man said as he poured the boiling water over the tea and set it on the stove to brew for a few minutes, setting the heat on low. "Most people don't know how much food is growing wild around them. I prefer some of them to store bought. We'll just wait a few minutes till the tea is ready."

The young folks listened and watched entranced as the old man rambled on. He reached up into the cupboard and took down a tin from the shelf. "My great granddaughter made me some biscuits yesterday, and I've been waiting for a special time to bring them out. I think this is the right time. It's mighty kind of you to come and visit an old man. I do like to have company drop by."

He got a plate out of the cupboard and piled it high with the biscuits, placing them on a small table in front of the young visitors. By this time the tea was ready to be served, so he poured a cup for each of them. He placed a pot of honey on the table beside the biscuits along with spoons and knives.

"Help yourselves, folks," he said. "Some people like honey in the tea and on the biscuits. I like honey on everything. My neighbour up the road, Johnny, has bees, and he brings me a pot every now and then."

Alex at the Interpretive Centre was right, Holly thought.

The chief continued talking, and when everyone was served, he finally pulled up a kitchen chair and sat down.

"I think I'm sitting in your chair, Mr. Chief," said Lorrie. "Here, I'll switch with you."

"Well, that's mighty thoughtful of you, girl. These old bones are sort of used to that chair." He got up and made the switch, using the remote to raise the foot rest. Then he gave a satisfied, toothless smile and said, "Now we talk."

The young sleuths all put honey in their tea and spread some on their biscuits. When they took the first sip of tea, there were, "umms" and "ahs" all around. The biscuits brought the same response. Their host responded with a toothless grin.

"This is wonderful," said Holly. "My mother would sure love to know how you make this tea, and the biscuits are scrumptious."

"Everybody wants my recipe for tea. Tell your mama to come see me, and I'll give it to her. But she'll have to go into the bush for the plants."

"I think she'd probably do that as long as Daddy went with her. Mom will do anything for a new recipe. Please tell your great granddaughter her biscuits are fantastic. Thank you for sharing them with us."

"Great granddaughter will be happy you like them. Now, what do you want to know about the slide and the mines?"

Holly told him about Susanna and their thoughts that the culprits might have hidden her in one of the mines.

"I saw a little red car go by a couple of days ago," the old chief told them. "I saw two fellas in it. Didn't see them come back, as it got a bit cold and I came back inside the cabin. You think they might've hidden her out here somewhere?"

"We're checking everywhere we think she might be stashed," said Ted. "We've been exploring caves, the bush, and even some old abandoned cabins at Crowsnest Lake."

"My grandson, Wolf, is a tracker. Would you like him to help you? He'll be coming here today with my supplies."

"I'm a tracker," said Ted. "If he's here before we leave Turtle Mountain, I'd sure like to talk to him. Maybe he can give us some ideas on where to look. We have several teams searching the Pass area, but if he wouldn't mind joining us, we'd sure like to have him. He'd be really welcome and a big help to us."

"Wolf knows all the mines in the Pass and could take you there," said the old chief. "His pappy—that's my son, Sky—is the chief now. He'll be retiring soon, and then Wolf will be the new chief. We need younger heads with new ideas to keep our history alive."

"Do you think he'd come with us?" Holly asked.

"If he's not working, he probably will," said the old chief. "I'd go if I could, but my old legs wouldn't get me far, and I'd just hold you back. My pappy worked in the mines since before the slide. In fact, he was working in the mine when the mountain fell down."

"We heard that. Would you tell us about it?" Paul asked.

"Well, my pappy was just a boy, fourteen years old. He worked for the miners as water boy and fetch and carry. This was long before I was born, but I heard the story a hundred times from my father. He thought he was going to die that night. If he had, I wouldn't have been born.

"It was the night shift. Some of the men had heard rumblings in the mountain, but they didn't pay much attention to it, because the mountain was known to rumble and groan a lot. My tribe, the Blackfoot, had warned the miners and the town of Frank that the mountain was walking all the time, and they expected it to fall down on the town. They called it, 'The Mountain that Moves.' They didn't know when it would happen, but they believed it would be soon.

"Nobody believed them, but on April 29th, 1903, around 4:00 in the mornin', there was a sound like a thousand cracks of thunder or cannons going off, and the whole side of the eastern slope of the mountain crashed down, wipin' out and buryin' three quarters of the town of Frank. Some of the boulders were the size of small apartment buildings. Only one little baby survived in that part of town … a little girl … but her whole family was wiped out. She lived well into her nineties. I knew her and her kids. At least seventy-six people died in their sleep. Everything in the runaway mountain's path disappeared from existence. A freight train had just crossed the bridge, and minutes later the bridge was wiped out.

"It disappeared into the Old Man River, which had become a lake. Hundreds of houses, tents, and people were ripped apart like twigs and flung across the valley and buried. Farms disappeared in seconds. In a minute and a half it was all over, except for the odd boulder that came crashin' down.

"More than a mile of the Canadian Pacific Railway was buried. Two survivors from the north side of town got lanterns and climbed over the mountain of rocks for three miles to stop a passenger train called the Spokane Flyer. It was full of passengers. One of the men had to give up from exhaustion, but the other man kept on, even after he injured his legs and back when he fell. He had to save the passengers from another tragedy, and he got there in time to stop the train and save the passengers.

"The survivors in the north end of the town had many injuries, but they were alive, and they helped anybody who needed help. But the miners were another story."

"Wow!" Holly exclaimed. "What about your father? How did he and the miners get out of the mine? Wasn't the mine in the mountain?"

"Yup," he said. "The miners were trapped. The mine entrance was blocked and had disappeared, and the men started to panic. Then one of the men took charge and ordered the men to get their tools, while the mine engineer tried to figure out how far they'd have to dig. They thought at first there would only be about thirty-five feet to the top. They were digging for their lives. Then the engineer figured out that it would be three hundred feet. No way out.

"That was when some of them started to give up. The oxygen supply was really low. They'd been singing songs to keep up their spirits, but now everybody was quiet as they tried to save the air. One of the men began to dig a new tunnel on another level where the engineer said there was a good chance they would be close to the surface, probably thirty feet.

"The men got a new spurt of hope and suddenly got their second wind, so they began to dig again. They worked in fifteen minute shifts, thinking that their efforts would be in vain, but thirteen hours after the slide had sealed them into a tomb in the mountain, they managed to break through. Miners are a real tough lot. Pappy said they never showed fear when they were buried alive, but the minute they were free, every one of them was crying. He said he was too. That's how Pappy told it to me," said the old chief. [4]

Holly could tell that the old man had told the story so many times that he knew every word by heart, and it was like a well refined monologue. There was a collective, explosive, "Wow!" from each of the young visitors. The expressions on their faces as old chief finished his story told how the true history had affected them.

"Stupendous! What an epic story," said Holly, "and you're a natural storyteller, Chief. You should write a book about it."

"Ah, I'd rather just tell people about it. I get more visitors that way." They got the toothless grin again. Suddenly, a man walked through the door. "Oh, there's Wolf now. Come and meet my new friends, Wolf."

"Hi there, folks. What have you been up to, Gramps? Every time I come here, you're having a party, and I wasn't invited." He was smiling as Paul introduced the young visitors, and he shook each of their hands.

---

[4] This account is based on historical fact.

"I don't think I've met any of you before. Do you live around here?" he asked, looking thoughtfully at Peggy and Lorrie. "Mmm … I believe I've seen you two young ladies in the Pass."

"Yes," said Peggy. "My sister and I live in Blairmore. The others are friends visiting from Vancouver. We're all camping at Crowsnest Lake. Your grandfather kindly invited us in for tea when we asked him to tell us about the slide and mines."

Wolf started to laugh. "I hope he didn't keep you too long. He likes to capture an audience so he can tell his story, and he bribes them with tea while he's on his soap box." His grandfather grinned at him.

"Oh, don't worry, Wolf. They came lookin' for me to hear the story. They're a nice group of young-uns, and they want to talk to you."

"Oh really? What can I do for you folks?"

"Well, your grandfather told us that you're a tracker," said Ted. "I'm a tracker too, but I don't know the area and could use some help. We have search and rescue teams working the lake and bush area, but we wanted to check out the hills around Turtle Mountain."

"What are you tracking?" asked Wolf.

Ted proceeded to tell Wolf about Susannah, and how his grandfather had seen a little red car go past on the trail a couple of days ago. He also said he and his friends thought she might be hidden in one of the boarded-up mines, and wondered if Wolf would be interested in helping them look. Since his grandfather had said he knew the mines' locations, they thought it would save time if they didn't have to search them out.

"Well, I do have some time off this week," said Wolf. "We've been waiting for some plumbing supplies to come in, and we can't continue the project till they get here. Dusty can get along without me for a couple of days. I'll come with you, if you don't mind waiting for about an hour, maybe less, till I go back to town and drop some plastic pipe off at the shop. I'll need to change into my hiking boots and pick up some warm clothes and tools that we might need, and I'll switch to my mountain bike. I also need to let my father, Sky, know where we're going."

"That's great," said Ted. "An hour will go by quickly. Your grandfather will keep us entertained with his stories."

"You're right about that," laughed Wolf.

"I'll make some more tea," said the old chief.

Wolf grinned. "He's happy to have the company. I'm off, and I won't be long."

The old chief was chuckling and almost skipping with glee as he darted around the kitchen and put the kettle on again. Holly was mesmerized at such energy in an old man, and she wondered just how old he was.

"Hang on to your mugs," he said. "There's more tea coming up. I'll make a different blend this time." He lifted down another can from the cupboard, rinsed out the teapot, put three spoonsful of loose tea in the pot, and settled down to wait for the kettle to boil again.

Holly was still curious about the aftermath of the mine disaster. She was horrified as she thought about how the survivors must have felt, cut off as they were from the roads, and the destruction of the railway. How they must have mourned their losses. She voiced her thoughts to the old Chief.

"How did the people who survived cope in the small corner of the town that was cut off from any outside help? With the railway destroyed, and the roads buried, how did they manage to take care of those who were left and those who were injured and needing medication?"

"My pappy said every man, woman, and young-un volunteered and took on a job to try to make the houses that were left livable. The women took care of the wounded and pooled their food to make it stretch. It was an impossible job to clear the massive boulders, so the men all took on the job of trying to make a trail around the slide.

"They made rafts to bring people over from the other side of the Old Man River, which was blocked and had turned into a lake. Since they were cut off, they didn't know that hundreds of volunteers from the other little towns around them were working to reach them by making new trails around the slide. People all came together, and even my tribe came out of the hills and pitched in."

"What did your father do when his job was finished in the mine? Did he go into another mine?" Bonnie asked.

"No. He was just a boy, and he didn't want to go back into the mines after he nearly died. The town folks called him a hero because he was so young, and the men said he worked as hard as they did when they were digging for freedom. All those men thought they were going to die in the mine, but they said my fourteen-year-old Pappy didn't whimper once—leastways till they were out and breathing fresh mountain air.

"A preacher man taught Pappy how to read and write. The town had to be rebuilt again, so Pappy worked in construction. He made sure all of us kids had an education and learned a trade or some other kind of work. My tribe has always called him a hero, since he helped to dig himself and the other miners out of the mine when he was only a boy. When he was twenty-five, he was named the new chief of our tribe. When he died in 1961, they made me the new chief, and when I turned seventy, I turned it over to my son, Sky. We need young minds to lead us to keep our people and our culture alive."

"You're an amazing man, Chief," said Ted. "I'm surprised that you relate the history of this mountain so eloquently while living alone up here in the hills, and you're so extremely perceptive. I can see you're also an educated man with a mind as clear as a bell, and I hope when I'm your age, my mind will be as sharp as yours. I'm with Holly on this one, Chief. Why don't you write a book about your tribe's relationship to the mountain's history? You'd be an overnight sensation."

"Yeah!" The kids showed their appreciation by applauding and agreeing with everything Ted had just said.

"Ah no, these old hands never learned to type," he said.

"I would buy your book," said Holly. "You could use a ghost writer. You're a teacher. We've all learned something from you today."

"None of my teachers are that interesting," said Paul. "I can't believe that so few people know about this catastrophe. It's one of the worst North American natural disasters ever, and should be in all the school history books."

"That's true," said Holly. "I wonder if the professor knows about it. He lived here for a while when he was young."

"We'll ask him when we get back to Blairmore," said Peggy. "I wonder if Dad knows the history. I'll never look at the Slide again without seeing the people being buried alive. It's like being on the inside looking through a foggy window as the world crashes and burns."

"It just goes to show you that you never know when you're going to die," said Holly. "One minute you're sleeping safe in your bed, and in the next second you're gone."

While Chief George was talking, he made the tea and passed it around. He brought another tin down from the cupboard. It was full of cookies, and he passed them around.

"We're eating all your supply of delicious sweets, Chief," said Holly.

"That's what they're here for," he chuckled. "Great granddaughter Cindy knows how much I like to make tea for company, and you can't have tea without something sweet, so she bakes for me at least once a week."

"Oh, this tea is wonderful," said Holly. "What do you call it?"

"Bring Mama out here for a visit and I'll tell you," he teased her.

"Well, that settles it," she said. "Mom just has to come and try your teas. I can't believe these recipes are from weeds and plants that grow all around us. Do you think they grow in B.C. too?"

"Dusty took me to a reservation in B.C. about twenty years ago," he said. "It was the Stwamish Reserve. We were visiting a friend of his from college, and we went on a gathering party. All the plants you need for these teas were there, same as here."

"That's terrific," Holly said. "The Stwamish Reservation is just a few miles up the road from where we live at Lions Bay. It's in Squamish. Daddy knows the chief there. He did some legal work for the reservation a couple of years ago."

"Is that right? Wait till I tell Dusty. He'll be real tickled. I'd better give Wolf a call and see what's keepin' him." The kids were surprised when he pulled out a cell phone.

"You have a phone?" said Paul, his eyebrows raised in surprise. "Up here in the hills, you have a phone?"

"Sure. My kids wouldn't let me stay here if they couldn't get a-hold of me. They're kinda funny that way." He was dialling as he spoke. "Hey, Wolf. You alright, boy? Oh, you're almost here? Good. See you in a few minutes. He's on the way," he said as he put the phone in his pocket. "Two minutes away. Oh, there he is."

They could hear the bike pull up outside the cabin, and soon Wolf walked through the door.

"Hi, everybody. I hope I didn't keep you waiting too long."

"No way," said Ted. "Your grandfather kept us entertained with his stories about the mountain and the Frank Slide. We told him he should write a book. With all his knowledge about the history of the disaster and the aftermath, it would be a runaway best seller."

"Yes, Gramps does keep the story alive. You're right, it shouldn't be forgotten. Do you have warm clothes with you? Sometimes the mountains get cold into the evening. We've got about four hours before we should come back down. Twilight can be very disorienting, and we don't want to get caught up there in the dark."

"Yes, we're always prepared for the weather," said Ted. "Our saddlebags are packed for any occasion. Our team is trained in search and rescue, except for Peggy and Lorrie, but they've been keeping up really well for the last couple of days, so I'm not worried that they'll have any problems. Holly and Bonnie have extra clothes that will fit them."

"Okay, then, let's go," said Wolf. "We don't know if these guys we're looking for are local or if they know the territory, but we'll check the mines on the next level first, since Gramps saw the car heading in that direction."

They said their goodbyes to the chief, who said he wished he was going with them. He wished them good luck and good hunting with a yearning look in his eyes.

Mines and Caves

CHAPTER 10

THE KIDS NOTICED THAT WOLF WAS CARRYING A RIFLE.

"Do you think you need the gun?" Holly asked.

"Better to be safe than sorry, like my dad always says. Where we're going, we might run into animals. Most of the time they'll stay away from humans, but you never know. And we don't know if the kidnappers are armed. It's best to be prepared. Don't worry, I have a license. I'm a deputy sheriff on the First Nations police force. My brother, Dusty, is a deputy sheriff too, and my father, Sky, is the First Nations' sheriff."

"What kind of animals?" Bonnie asked, with a little hint of fear and trepidation in her voice. "Not wolves, I hope."

"Could be," said Wolf, "but don't worry. I know how to scare them off. I've lived in these mountains all my life, and I know how to live with the animals. Remember, my name is Wolf. There's a reason for that. The wolves like me. I used to have one as a pet."

"Really?" Holly was flabbergasted. "Don't you worry about your grandfather living out here all by himself at his age?" Holly asked.

Wolf laughed. "Nobody tells Gramps what to do. He built that cabin and has lived there all his life. He and Grandma raised five kids there. That's where he feels like he belongs. He's never alone, at least not for long. His old friend, Johnny Whitefeather, lives in the cabin just up the road from him.

"You didn't see Johnny's cabin. It's hidden in the trees, but they spend half their day sitting in old rocking chairs on the porch shooting the breeze. Johnny keeps bees. That's where Gramps gets his honey.

"They were the number one trackers in all of the Pass area when they were younger. Now they're content to sit and just talk about it. Somebody from the family always comes out twice a day to check on him, but he always has folks from town visiting and having tea with him, so he's never alone."

"How old is the chief?" Holly asked. "He seems so ancient, but he's really fast on his feet."

Wolf laughed. "He is ancient! He'll be 102 next month. I keep thinking I should leave him something in my will, because he might outlive all of us. He thinks he's part of the landscape."

They'd been riding slowly, with Wolf riding close beside the girls. They all had a good laugh about the will joke. Suddenly Wolf took a right turn and headed into the bush. He raised his hand and stopped them and got off his bike. Ted joined him while they inspected the faint trail.

"They wouldn't be able to bring a car in here, but they could have parked it and walked in. I don't see any signs that they've been here, but stay close," he said. "And follow me. There's a cave in here I think we should look at before we head up to the mine."

"I don't see any recent signs either," said Ted, "but I think you're right. We should take a look. They might have gone in by another trail."

"Let's hide our bikes in the bush and walk in," said Wolf. "Just in case the kidnappers drive out here, we don't want them to know we're here, so hide them real well with branches and bushes for camouflage."

"We have chains and padlocks as well," said Paul. "We don't want to take a chance on the thieves stealing even one of our top-of-the-line bikes. They were a gift from our benefactor, our adopted uncle. Well, he kind of adopted us when we saved him and his wife from drowning, and we'd never be able to replace them. The thieves already stole one bike along with two canoes and motors and other items as well as the car."

"And don't forget Susannah," said Peggy. "They stole her too."

"It looks like they're piling up quite a rap sheet," said Wolf. "But when they steal a girl, the law won't stop looking for them. That's kidnapping. Since Susannah's been missing since Sunday, she might be in real bad shape when we find her, but one way or the other, we'll find her. Let's hope she's still alive. We can't let these scumbags get away with it."

The young searchers followed Wolf and Ted along the trail. Wolf had a large knife, like a machete, and Ted had a hunter's knife. They slashed and hacked away at the thick bushes and entangled tree branches to make a path through the bush.

"They didn't come in this way if they went to the cave," said Wolf. "There's another trail further up, and it's probably easier to reach the cave from there. This trail is so congested, they probably don't know about it or wouldn't take it if they did. Nobody's been along here in years, not even the animals. That's good, because if the perps are in there, they won't be expecting us."

"Is it very far?" Lorrie asked.

"No, it just feels like it is because we're fighting our way through this jungle of brush and weeds," Wolf told her. "Just hang in there. You're all doing great!"

They'd followed Wolf and Ted for another twenty minutes or so when Wolf told them to be very quiet, as they were getting close to the cave. There wasn't a sound out of any of them as they crept to the edge of the clearing. They could see the cave through the trees at the other side of the clearing. It was almost covered with brush, but they could see enough of it to know they'd arrived.

Wolf touched his lips with his finger to warn them all to be quiet. Then he pointed to Ted and indicated with a wide sweep of his hand that he should use the thick fir trees around the edge of the clearing for cover. He would then make his way in a half circle to the left of the cave entrance where he would have cover from a large spruce. He whispered some instructions into his ear. Ted almost laughed out loud. This would be fun.

Wolf whispered the same instructions to Paul, indicting he should take the right side of the clearing and work his way around to that side of the cave entrance, taking cover behind some bushes by the entrance. The two guys grinned at the scenario he was setting up.

He whispered to the girls to stay put and explained what he was going to do. He also told them not to come out from the cover of the trees no matter what they saw. Then he took an empty whiskey bottle and a water flask full of his grandfather's tea from his backpack and poured some tea from the flask into the whiskey bottle. They still hadn't seen any activity from the cave. He pulled a poncho style Native blanket from his backpack and pulled it over his shoulders, wrapping it around him, and added an old beat up hat.

He turned to the girls and again touched his fingers to his lips to indicate silence. Then he signalled to each of the guys to start around on their journey to the cave. He waited until he saw them wave from their assigned spots, and then he staggered out into the clearing, singing an old Native chant and performing a rain dance ... or a war dance. The kids weren't sure which, but they were mesmerized as they watched. Every now and then he would stop and take a drink of tea from the whiskey bottle, wave the bottle around like an old drunk, and then begin the dancing and chanting again.

This went on for about ten minutes, but it hadn't drawn any attention from the cave. Wolf danced closer and closer to the entrance, and when he realized his drunken performance hadn't brought the expected audience, he stopped dancing and went into the cave with his pistol drawn. He came back out almost immediately.

"Sorry guys," he said. "There's nobody in there, but it was a good first rehearsal. We'll use this scenario at every mine or cave we stop at. If they're there, they'll just think it's a drunken old Blackfoot, and they'll probably come out to take a look. Don't worry, we'll find them."

"That was amazing," said Holly, and they all applauded. "You were so believable. I would have come out of the cave to watch you. It was so entertaining. You must have done this before."

"A few times, when Sky and I were chasing some bad guys, we coaxed them out of hiding this way. They never caught on until we had the handcuffs on them."

"What do we do now?" asked Paul.

"Well, fortunately we've cut a path in here, so it won't be so tough getting out," said Wolf. "Let's go. We don't want to waste the daylight hours. We'll take the same trail back."

The young hunters didn't argue. They followed Wolf and Ted much more quickly on the trip back. Their bikes hadn't been touched. The branches and bushes they'd used to cover them hadn't been moved. Wolf pointed to a slope about eight hundred feet away.

"See that ledge up there? We have to climb up there to get to the old Black Rock Mine. The only way they'd be able to get the girl up there, if she's there, is if she climbed up herself. If they were threatening her, she probably could do it, but she'd have to be in pretty good shape. We could try that one first, if you like, or we could go on farther up the trail to the Rusty Bucket Mine."

"Which one do you think we should try first?" Ted asked. "Which one do you think would be the most likely choice for the kidnappers?"

"Well, the Rusty Bucket would be the easiest one to access. They could probably drive the car closer to it, and for that reason, they might choose it. We could drive right up to it on the bikes. It's been broken into before by a bunch of bikers. Black Rock is quite a climb. Your choice."

"Let's take the easy road first," said Holly. "These guys might just be crazy enough to think nobody will bother to follow them up the mountain, so they'd choose the first hidey hole they could find. Climbing up a steep slope with a hostage might not appeal to them. Besides, what would they do with the car?"

"You might be right," said Wolf. "What about the rest of you? Do you want to go for The Rusty Bucket, or do you want to climb?"

The group discussed it for a few minutes, and then ended up deciding to head for The Rusty Bucket Mine.

"Okay, guys. Follow me," said Wolf. "It looks like it might rain, and it's getting a bit cold, so let's roll. Even with the bikes, it's slow moving uphill, but we'll ride as far as we can."

They all climbed onto their bikes and Wolf led the way. "There's also another cave at the bluff," he told them, "so if we're caught in the rain, we'll have shelter."

"We have lots of rainwear with us," said Holly.

"That's good," said Wolf. "I think you're going to need it."

"Oh, look," said Bonnie. "There's a whole family of deer hiding in the bushes over there. Aw, look at the babies. Aren't they adorable?"

"Yeah, they're curious, but they won't come out of the bushes while we're here. They don't trust humans," Wolf said. "And you can't really blame them. When the hunters come up here, the animals all head for the high crags and bluffs where they can hide."

"But we're not here to shoot them," said Lorrie. "They don't need to hide from us, especially not the little Bambis."

"Well, they don't exactly know that. They feel pretty safe right now, but they seem to know when the hunters come hunting for them. It's not hunting season yet, but when it is, the animals go into hiding, and they climb as far as they can up the rocky mountain to the safety of the caves, clefts, and crags at the top."

The riders rode in silence for a while. Wolf knew the terrain and helped them to avoid the really bad spots. Their bikes were the very best that Harvey Fields' money could buy, and they were solidly equipped for mountain riding. Their young owners treated them with kid gloves. They took very good care of all the much-appreciated equipment their benefactor bestowed on them.

The bikes rode like Cadillacs over the rough terrain, and they'd been riding about fifteen minutes when Wolf turned off the main trail to the right. There was a recognizable trail, and it looked like it might have been used recently. It wasn't as difficult to follow as the one to the cave, as it didn't have as many low bushes.

Trees lined the worn path, and they drove the bikes in about six hundred yards, and then Wolf raised his hand like he had before. They stopped and he warned them to be quiet by touching his finger to his mouth. He used his hands to call them towards him, and then in just above a whisper, he told them they were close to the mine.

"We'll leave the bikes here. Hide them in the trees, and we'll use the same scenario as we did before. Ted will take the left side, and Paul the right. Stay well back under cover of the trees till you get to the entrance and hide behind the bushes. I'll do my thing, and if it draws them out of the mine, you two guys jump out and grab them. I'll hold them with my gun, and you can cuff them. Any questions?"

"Do we have the authority to cuff them?" asked Ted. "We're not law enforcement."

"Right! Very insightful, Ted. Okay, Ted and Paul, raise your right hands." They did so. "What's your last names?" They told him and he continued. "Okay. Ted Lumley and Paul Castles, by the power invested in me by the First Nations Police Force, I now deputized you both. You are now First Nations Police deputies, and will work under my supervision on this mission. Now let's get to work. Follow my lead and my signals."

The group all grinned and gave Paul and Ted, a thumbs up. Wolf told them all to follow him. When they reached the clearing, he signalled to the girls to stay and hide behind the trees. Ted and Paul followed his directions to the letter and moved like wraiths through the trees to their spots beside the entrance and back just a little behind the bushes. When they were in place, they raised their arms to indicate they'd arrived at their appointed spot.

Wolf donned his cape blanket and pulled the decrepit old hat down on his head. The whiskey bottle still had some of his grandfather's tea in it, and he was set to go.

"Showtime," he whispered to the girls as he set off on his drunken act. He burst through the trees singing his chant and waving the bottle as he danced the rain dance or whatever mesmerizing contortion it was. The girls watched as they giggled and shook with silent laughter, knowing they couldn't make a sound.

Wolf knew how to command the stage. His circle got wider and wider until he was almost to the mine. If there was anyone in there, they weren't paying attention. Wolf kept the act up until he was at the mine, and then he went inside. Ted and Paul followed him, and they turned on their zoom flashlights.

"I think we've hit a no-show again," said Wolf.

"Yeah, I think you're right," said Paul, "but it does look like someone's been here lately."

"Right," Wolf agreed. "Here's some recent garbage they've left behind. It must have been very recent, because the rats haven't even been into it yet."

"I thought Alberta didn't have any rats," said Ted.

"Oh, there are rats here, just not so many," explained Wolf.

Paul and Ted shone their flashlights into the back of the mine and walked tentatively along the tracks.

"There's a room over there." Ted pointed his light to the right. "Probably used as an office for the mine. We should check it out."

"Be careful," Wolf warned them. "It's probably not safe in here. It's supposed to be boarded up, but somebody has definitely broken in. Just be careful where you step. The beams are all rotting and it could fall in on you at any minute, or you could fall through the rotten boards into a shaft. I don't want to lose my two new deputies on their first day."

The zoom flashlights lit up the tunnel, but the guys remembered what it was like in the mine in Garibaldi Mountain and wondered what would happen to them if the lights died out. They stepped slowly towards the door, which was hanging off the hinges, being careful to pick their steps and test their weight on the rotting boards. Ted went through the door first and shone his light around. There was still an old desk and a couple of chairs that had been left behind when the mine closed.

"It doesn't look like they were planning to close down," said Ted. "Come on in, Paul, and shine your flashlight to the other side of the room. They left a pile of something over there in the corner. What is it?"

Paul shone his flashlight on the pile, and suddenly it moved. The guys jumped back, thinking it might be an animal, but soon they heard a moaning, whimpering sound coming from the pile.

"Hold it, guys," Wolf warned. "Shine your light over here too, Ted." As he spoke, he shone his own flashlight on the bundle.

Wolf pulled out his gun and walked slowly over to the pile. There was another moaning sound, and Wolf grabbed the material and quickly pulled it back. A pair of frightened blue eyes, full of tears, blinked at the lights blinding her.

"No, please, no," she pleaded.

"Good Lord above!" Wolf exclaimed. "We've found her, and she's tied hands and feet so tight her circulation is cut off." He pulled out a knife to cut the ropes. "Don't worry, Susannah. We're not the kidnappers. We're here to help you. I'm from the police. My name is Deputy Sheriff

Wolf Rivers," he said in a kindly voice as he motioned to Paul and Ted. "Please call the girls. Tell them to bring blankets and water. I'll phone the First Nations police and an ambulance."

He had to step outside the mine to make the call. When he got Sky on the line, he said, "We've found the girl, and we need a doctor and a stretcher to get her down the trail to the ambulance. This girl is in bad shape. I want whoever did this to her caught before they can hurt another girl. Call in whatever help you can find."

"Don't worry, Wolf," said Sky. "Cliff's here, and he's calling for the Medic-copter. They'll be there in a few minutes, and they'll land right beside the Rusty Bucket. Don't move her. The medics will do that."

He went back into the mine. The girls had already arrived. Holly was trying to give Susannah some water from her flask without much success. The girl was barely conscious and unable to respond to their well-meaning help and questions, except with moans and whimpers.

"It's best if you don't try to question her. Let the medical professionals and the police detectives do that. I'd like to get her out of here," said Wolf. "The mine is dangerous, but it might be just as dangerous to move her. We don't know what injuries she has, and you're not supposed to move someone in her condition until she's been examined by a doctor. We're going to have to wait for the Medic-copter."

"We were told you didn't have a detective in the Pass," said Holly. "My father's a detective, and he's also a lawyer. I'm sure he'd be willing to help in any way he could. He's at the camp in Blairmore."

"What's his cell number? We just might need him," said Wolf.

Holly gave him the number along with her father's name and the name of his firm in Vancouver in case he needed to check him out. Wolf called his father, the sheriff, again.

"Hi, Sky. Holly just told me her father's a legal detective. He's at the campground in Blairmore. Maybe you should give him a call and ask him to consult with us."

"Yeah, that's a good idea. We need some legal advice here. I'll call Cliff back. Give me the detective's name and number. We really need to hire a detective for the Pass again. Having to call someone in from Calgary every time we need their expertise is not good enough. Cliff sent two guards out with the copter just in case those two guys come back. They'll stay there for a couple of days."

"Hey, I hear the 'copter. They're here," Wolf said. "That was fast. I'd better go and get the kids. See you at the hospital in thirty minutes."

The helicopter landed right beside the mine entrance. Two medics and a nurse got out, and old Doc Winters followed them at a slower pace. The two guards pulled a fold-up stretcher out of the back. The medics grabbed on to it and ran with it into the mine entrance. Wolf had to tell them to step carefully and to watch out for rotting boards. That slowed them down a bit, so the young explorers all zoomed their flashlights into the room. Ordinarily they'd have been asked to leave, but light was needed. They were told to stand back, so they zoomed the light at the victim. The guys turned their heads away out of respect.

The nurse and medics worked swiftly. In no time at all, they had Susannah hooked up to portable machines and were checking her vitals and inspecting the wounds and bruises all over her poor broken body. The old doc kept shaking his head and muttering to himself.

"Poor little girl," he said. "What kind of animals would do this? We need to move her to the hospital immediately. We can finish checking her out on the way. She'll need X-rays to show us the extent of her injuries. Let's get her out of here."

The nurse and medics packed up quickly and transferred her to the stretcher. She moaned and cried as they moved her, but once she was on the stretcher, they had her in the helicopter in less than five minutes. The helicopter took off, and the young rescuers watched it disappear over the trees.

"Don't worry," said Wolf. "She'll be at the hospital in five minutes, and they'll take real good care of her."

"Where are the guards going to stay for the next two days?" asked Holly. "The mine is too dangerous for them to stay in there."

"They brought a tent with them in the helicopter, and they'll set up in the trees behind the mine. They won't be seen from the trail if the perps show up. Don't worry, the guards are used to roughing it. They have supplies with them, so they won't starve," said Wolf. "They're always prepared to go at a moment's notice, so they'll be fine."

"Oh, that's good," said Holly. "I thought I was going to have to leave them my duffle bag."

"And why would you leave them your duffle bag?" asked Wolf.

The guys burst out laughing. "Holly thinks she has to feed the world," said Paul, "so she carries a duffle bag full of food in her saddlebag. Nobody goes hungry when they travel with Holly. Her mom keeps her fridge full just so she can raid it."

"It would be good to check out the duffle bag, but I think we should get going. I want to get to the hospital as quickly as possible, so let's hit the trail," Wolf suggested.

This time when they mounted the bikes, they moved at a faster pace. Wolf phoned the old chief while they were on the way to let him know they'd found the girl. As they passed the cabin, they saw the chief and Johnny on the porch waving at them to show their delight at their success. Holly waved and promised to bring her mom to visit and have some of his tea. He grinned and nodded and clapped his hands in glee.

As they turned off the mountain road onto the highway they picked up the pace, and they were soon rolling into Blairmore. Wolf led them straight to the hospital, where they parked beside two police cruisers. Holly's father and the professor were already there.

They were in conference with the doctors and officers Cliff and Roland. Sheriff Sky Rivers, Wolf's father, was also in the group. Wolf joined them, and the sheriff introduced him to Detective Brannigan and the professor. It was obvious from the grave looks on their faces that they were discussing Susannah's case, and that the results of their examinations were serious. The young rescuers waited patiently for them to finish their discussion, and then Wolf called them over and introduced them to his father, Sky, and the doctors.

"We probably wouldn't have found her in time," he said, "if these young folks hadn't volunteered to pursue the case. They deserve a medal for their tenacity. It was their idea to search the caves and mines that led to finding Susannah. Now we have to search for the scoundrels who kidnapped her.

"They also have her car and belongings, and they've been committing multiple robberies all through the Pass. This is the first time we've heard of them kidnapping or assaulting anyone, or attempting murder. What they did to that girl was attempted murder. She wouldn't have made it if she'd been left there another day. If they don't go back to the mine, then we know they left her there to die."

"We're turning this investigation over to Detective Brannigan," said the sheriff. "He's kindly offered his help, and we gladly accepted it. We do our best here, and we usually don't need a detective, but this case goes beyond the petty crimes we're accustomed to here in the Pass."

"I'm glad to help," said David, "and the search will continue. Our volunteers will not be happy until the criminals are found. They have to be hiding out somewhere in the Pass. Wolf, you said the garbage you found at the cave was recently put there, and your father saw the car go by yesterday, so they just might go back there. If they do, the guards will get them. Ask your father to call you if he sees the car again."

"Oh, don't worry, he definitely will. He's as interested in this case as we are. If he was younger, he and Johnny Whitefeather would be out there searching for the perps."

The doctors permitted Holly and her team to go into Susannah's room two at a time, since they were responsible for saving her. Holly and Paul went in first. Holly placed her hand over her mouth when she saw the poor wounded girl in the bed. One leg and both arms were in casts, which indicated broken bones, and her neck was in a brace. The bruises on her face were terrible to see, and her other leg was bruised from the ankle up to the knee brace.

"Oh, poor Susannah," said Holly as she touched her swollen hand so gently. "How could they have done this to you?" She didn't know if Susannah could hear her, as she was heavily medicated. "We'll find those monsters," she promised, "and we'll find your car. They'll be punished severely. I'll be praying that you get well quickly. Dear God in heaven, please take care of Susannah and make her well again," she offered up in a short prayer.

"We'll find them," said Paul. "There's nowhere they can go that we won't find them. And don't worry, Susannah, Holly and I and our friends are teaching your class to swim. When you're well again, we'd like to invite you to come and visit us at the coast, and we'll teach you to scuba dive."

"Absolutely," said Holly. "You can come to my house and stay as long as you like to recuperate. I live in Lions Bay."

There were tears in Holly's eyes. Susannah didn't make any sign that she'd heard them, but as they were saying goodbye, Holly felt a faint little squeeze on her hand.

"Oh, I think she heard us," Holly said tearfully. "She squeezed my hand, just a little. I think she's going to be alright."

They left the room and told Bonnie and Ted what happened, encouraging them to go in. It was much the same for them as well. They, like Holly, were at the point of crying when they saw the damage that had been done to this poor girl, and they blamed themselves for not getting to the mine sooner. Bonnie stroked her head, trying to find a spot that hadn't been injured. She too felt that Susannah heard them.

"We'll come back tomorrow," Bonnie said. "I'll pray that you'll be feeling much better."

Peggy and Lorrie went in next. They only stayed a couple of minutes. Lorrie was crying when they came out. She said she couldn't bear to think that the perpetrators were probably from the Pass area and were roaming free, thinking they wouldn't be caught.

"I want to see Mom and Dad," she said. "Let's go to their camp and have dinner with them. They'll want to know about Susannah anyway."

"Good idea," said Holly. "I'm going to phone Andy to let him know we found her and to tell him we'll fill him in later on this evening."

Just then, Holly's father and the professor joined them. Holly told them they were going to the campground to see the family and have dinner with them.

"That's good," her father said. "They're all just as interested in how the rescue turned out as we are. I must phone Milton and Phil to bring them up to date on the success of the search. They'll |inform the others. Don't forget, we're only half finished. The perpetrators are still at large.

"They must be holed up somewhere, because there's an APB out on them, and the police patrols are stopping any little red sports cars driving on the number three highway. Of course, they could be up in the hills somewhere. That little car is equipped with four-wheel drive and could drive almost anywhere. I hope those criminals haven't ruined it. Susannah has suffered so much. We've managed to track down her parents, and they're on their way."

"Oh, thank goodness for that," said Holly. "Susannah really needs her parents right now. Anyway, we're heading for the campground. I want to hug my mother. Now I know why she worries so much about me when I'm off on my travels."

"I know she worries," said her father, "but I know that when you're with Paul, Ted, and Bonnie you're as safe as you could possibly be, and I'm always at the end of your phone with the National Guard if they're needed."

"What more could a girl ask for?" she laughed.

"Well, your mother would like to keep you wrapped up in swaddling clothes till you're at least thirty." He was laughing at the thought as he said it.

The group was tired. It had been a frightening experience for them, and they were glad to end the day's search with results, even if they weren't happy results. Susannah's injuries would take a long time to heal—probably even as much as a year. There would be months of rehab from what they could see, and they'd heard the nurses talking in whispers about broken ribs as well.

Susannah looked like she'd been through a war. It was a very nice hospital, and she was getting the best of care, but Holly remembered a friend telling her that when you're injured with broken bones, no matter how well you're cared for, you're never the same again. She was inclined to believe that, because her friend still walked with a limp, and her back always hurt, even after five years. Susannah's injuries were so extensive, and she was only twenty-two. Would she be disabled all her life?

When they pulled into the campground, Willie came running to meet them. He was excited, as usual.

"Hi, Ted! Hi, Paul!" he shouted as he ran alongside the bikes. "I was swimming in the river today," he shouted. "Dad too! I did the breast stroke and the crawl. Me and Dad, we had a race. I won!"

"Super cool, Willie!" said Ted.

They parked the bikes and joined the family at the extended table to cries of welcome and questions about the search. First of all, Holly, Peggy, and Lorrie ran up to their mothers and gave them hugs.

"Is anything wrong?" Susan asked, wondering at the sudden display of affection. The twins' mother was asking the same question.

"No, nothing's wrong," said Holly. "We just want you to know we love you and appreciate you. Now I know why you worry so much about me."

"Now I know something's wrong," said Kate.

"Well, we have some news," said Holly. "We found Susannah!"

"And where was she? Is she alive? Was she in an accident?" The questions were coming so fast, Holly finally held up her hand so she could speak.

"She's alive, but in very bad shape," she said. "She's in the hospital."

David Brannigan and the professor pulled into the campground and parked their bikes. As they sat down, they fielded questions fast and furiously. Finally, David stopped the chatter by holding up his hand and turning the questions over to Holly's team.

"Holly and her group have been on this case all day. They have all the answers. I've just been asked to investigate by the local police and the First Nations police force. Holly and her group can tell you how they found Susannah. I haven't had a chance to talk to them yet, so let them tell you how they discovered the girl."

"Okay, Holly. Let's have it," said Heather. "We're all ears."

"Well, Officer Cliff told us that Susannah's car had been spotted in the town of Frank. We wanted to go to Frank anyway to see the Slide. When we got there, we were overwhelmed by the destruction to the town. Three quarters of the town was buried in a minute and a half.

The manager of the Interpretive Centre told us some of the story, but Andy had told us about old Chief George Rivers. He said he knew more about the history of the Slide than anybody else in town, because his father was working in the mine when the mountain came down. Ted had a map Andy had given him, so we decided to go to the chief's cabin and talk to him. Ted could tell you more about the trail," she said.

Ted picked up the story. "It was pretty rough going," he said. "If you lived there, you'd need a truck to handle the holes and ruts. We followed the map, and it took us about twenty minutes to reach the old chief's cabin. It was set back in the trees, and it was pretty old. Wolf said the old chief had built it and raised five kids there."

Holly picked the story up again. She told the group about old Chief George, and related how they met his son, Wolf. Her audience enjoyed the tale of how Wolf acted drunk to draw out the perps, but they grew silent again as she described how they found Susannah and the terrible state she was in.

"That poor girl," said Susan. "Has her family been notified?"

"Yes, they were on their way when we left the hospital. Susannah has multiple broken bones. I don't know what those guys did to her, but they must have beaten her with two by fours. We cried when we saw her. We just have to find the perpetrators and bring them to justice. I'm glad Daddy's on the case. The police here said they really need him, and they'll do whatever he suggests."

"And I'm available to help you, David, in any way I can," said Gordon. "I do know this countryside, so that may be to our advantage. I have some ideas from my youth about where they might hole up to hide. Let's arrange a meeting with the other search team leaders after dinner."

"Good idea," said David. "We need to make a plan. I'll ask Cliff and Sky if they know of a sketch artist who could maybe draw a picture of these two hoodlums from a witness's description. The old chief and Johnny Whitefeather both saw them in the car yesterday. It was probably just a glimpse, but from your description of the old chief, he sounds like he doesn't miss much. Maybe between the two of them we'll get a description, or even a partial description, which would help us identify them. The perps might hide the car for now, but they'll have to shop for food. I wonder if they found any prints at the cabin and boathouse where they stashed the canoes and other items, or if they discovered which fast food restaurant they were buying their take-outs from. We might get a description from whoever served them there. I'll have a talk with Cliff.

"We need to get a team out to the mine to check for prints as well, but we don't want to draw attention to the mine till we see if they come back to the scene of the crime. Okay, let's eat. We have a lot to follow up on before we sleep tonight."

"Dinner's ready everybody," Susan said. "Take your seats around the table. You can hash everything out while you're eating."

More than twenty people pulled up to the table, which consisted of four picnic tables pulled together and covered with white plastic tablecloths. The tables were groaning with food. Susan was in her element, as cooking was one of her favourite things to do, and Heather was her right-hand helper. The ladies were afraid they'd miss one word of the plans the men were putting together.

"By the way, David," said Phil, "I happen to know a sketch artist. She's very good and has sometimes helped the police by sketching a perpetrator from a witness's description. She lives here in the Pass. Would you like me to call her?"

"Definitely," said David. "Could you ask her to join us here for dinner?"

"Yes, do," said Susan. "There's plenty of food … enough for an army."

"Her name is Candace McIver. She's an art teacher at the high school," Phil said as he pulled his phone out. "I'll call her now."

"Candace is a nice lady," said Kate. "She's on the town council and is one of my good friends. She never takes time to cook, so she'll definitely be here for dinner. Her condo is just around the corner."

"She said she'll be right over," said Phil. "Okay, let's eat. Just make sure you leave her some."

They were still passing the food around when Candace arrived. She really did live just around the corner. Susan had made sure there was a place setting for her, and she sat down beside Holly and across from David and Gordon. Phil introduced them, and after the introductions were carried out around the table, David filled her in on what they required of her.

"I know the old chief," she said. "He's pretty savvy, and I love his teas. I drop in every once in a while for a cup."

"Even better," said David. "You'll have a good rapport with him then, and it will be so much easier to work together, since you're already acquainted."

"Oh yes," said Holly. "I almost forgot, Mom … I promised the old chief I'd take you to have tea with him. The teas are to die for. He said he'd give you the recipes if you came."

"Then I'll have to go," she said. "Heather will come also."

"We could go out there tomorrow, if you like," Candace offered. "I'm off work till next week. That's when school starts. Then I'm really tied up, especially during the first semester. I have old chief's phone number if you'd like me to call him and tell him we're coming."

"I hope he'll be open to cooperating with us," said David.

She laughed. "You obviously don't know the old chief. He'll be positively delighted. If you haven't met him, you're in for a treat."

"I'll be taking Susan on the back of my bike," said David, "and Gordon will be taking Heather. I'll call Wolf and ask him to take you on his bike, Candace."

"Oh, no need," said Candace. "I have a very nice mountain bike I like to ride in the summer. I've been to the old chief's cabin many times. His teas are worth the ride. I always take him something sweet. He always says it's for his sweet tooth, but that's a joke, because he doesn't have any teeth."

"Oh, then maybe Magen could ride with you," suggested Holly. "We couldn't take her yesterday, as we didn't have room on our bikes. Sorry about that, Magen."

"Certainly," said Candace. "She can ride with me."

"Thank you, Candace," said Magen.

"Wolf will want to go anyway to check on his grandfather and see the sketch, so I'll call him and fill him in," said David. "He'll probably want to check in with the guards at the mine as well. So far, there's been no word that the perps have shown up. We'll leave here at 9:00 a.m., so try to be here a few minutes before that. Since he's an elderly man, I would assume he doesn't rise too early in the morning."

Candace laughed. "Old Chief is up with the sun. He could teach us a thing or two about wasting the day, and he probably will. Around here, they treat him like a national icon."

"From what you've all told me about him, I think he's probably the one I'll remember the most. I'm looking forward to meeting him," said David. Gordon repeated his sentiments.

"We'll head out to the lake camp and give Andy an update," said Holly. "We'll also have to reschedule the class for the afternoon. The kids need a little more instruction, so they'll feel safe. After that, all they need is practice. I think we can spare an hour in the afternoon."

The Mountain Search Continues

CHAPTER 11

WHEN THEY PULLED INTO THE LAKE, THE WHOLE CAMP TURNED OUT TO MEET them. In his excitement, and in his mad dash to meet them, Socrates kept tumbling over himself. As usual, he made a huge lunge for Holly, almost knocking her down, to show his affection by licking her to death.

"Stop that, Socrates!" Holly shouted. But Socrates wasn't listening. He was determined to show Holly how much he missed her. "Paul, get him off me," she pleaded. Paul and all the other kids were so busy laughing at the display of love that they didn't immediately jump to attention.

"I'm glad it's you he loves," said Bonnie as she doubled over with the giggles.

"Well, I wish he didn't love me so much," said Holly as Socrates was finally calmed down by Paul. "Look at my clothes. I'm covered in slime. Okay, Socrates, I love you too. Just lie down and be a good dog." She petted him to let him know she wasn't mad at him.

Andy was laughing along with everybody else. Now he got serious. "Okay, tell us what's been happening. We've been waiting on pins and needles for some news."

"Oh, did Officer Cliff not phone and tell you?" said Holly. "We found Susannah. She's in the hospital in very bad shape."

"What happened?" gasped Andy. "Was she in an accident?"

"No, she wasn't in an accident. She met some really bad guys." Holly told them the whole story to gasps of horror from the staff and campers. "If we hadn't found her when we did, the doctors said she would have died. As it is, she's going to wish she'd died before she gets better. She's suffering from multiple broken bones in her legs, arms, and ribs, and she sustained head wounds. There isn't any place she wasn't beaten. The weapons they used must have been two by fours or baseball bats. The police said they'd never seen anyone so badly beaten in all their years on the force."

"What kind of monsters would do that to a girl?" Andy fumed. "Do they know who these perpetrators are?"

"Not yet, but they're taking fingerprints and checking where they might have bought take out food. I noticed you got your canoes back. Did the police bring all the other stuff back?"

"Not yet. They're printing them and sorting to see who owns them. They said they might have to hold them for evidence. The only reason I got the canoes was that they didn't have any place to store them, so they said they'd be safer here. They'd already printed them, and they're just waiting for the results. I've put chains on them to hold them for evidence, but this is the first news we've heard about Susannah. God help her."

"Another thing," said Paul. "We have to reschedule the class and change it to the afternoon. Tell the kids to be ready by two o'clock. If anything changes, we'll phone."

"We're going to bed early tonight," said Holly. "The search teams all have to meet in Blairmore at 9:00 a.m. It's been a long day."

"Yes, it has," said Andy. "You've had a long day. Can I get you anything? A hot chocolate maybe?"

They all declined and headed for their tents.

"I'm exhausted," said Bonnie. The young explorers all agreed with her. Nobody wanted to stay up and sing.

As soon as their heads hit the pillows, they were all asleep. Socrates flopped contentedly between Holly and Bonnie's sleeping bags, and before long was snoring and whimpering in his dreams. There was a light mist over the lake and a warm chinook wind blowing in from the West Coast, but the expected storm didn't arrive.

Holly's watch alarm went off all too soon. She nudged Bonnie and received the expected groan for her efforts.

"Come on, Sleeping Beauty. Time to get up."

"What time is it?" Bonnie's eyes squinted over the edge of the sleeping bag. "We just came to bed."

"It's seven thirty-five. We have to eat breakfast and be in Blairmore by eight-fifty. I'll get breakfast ready while you go and waken the rest of the tribe. Tell them breakfast will be ready in fifteen minutes."

Bonnie was dressing as she spoke. "Why do we always have to be the ones who get up first?"

Holly laughed. "Five extra minutes isn't going to help one way or the other. I'm off to the kitchen to get the duffle bag out of the cooler. Do you want coffee, tea, or milk?"

"Milk preferably, but I'm good with whatever's available." Bonnie headed out to waken the others while Holly headed for the camp kitchen. Soon there were audible groans and moans from the other tents. Charlie and Sally stayed in their sleeping bags, as they didn't need to get up till later. They said they would scuba dive and explore to put in the time until the group came back to the lake for the class.

"Are you sure?" said Holly. "Because you could ride into the Blairmore camp on the back of Paul and Ted's bikes."

"No, that's fine," said Sally. "We like being by the lake."

Peggy and Lorrie didn't put up too much of a fuss when Bonnie wakened them. It seemed like they were accustomed to getting ready in a hurry, because by the time Holly came back from the kitchen, they were dressed and offering to help. Holly laid all the food out on the picnic table and told everybody to just help themselves. Peggy and Lorrie brought milk and hot chocolate from the kitchen. Andy was already up and was fussing around them.

"I want to say thank you to all of you for finding, Susannah," he said. "I think it was an intervention by God that brought you to our campground. You will always be welcome here, with or without a reservation."

"Thank you, Andy. We'll feel much better when we find the criminals who caused so much trouble for you and Susannah. Don't worry," Holly said, "the police are on the ball, and they'll be caught. We're going to work with them till the end of the week, and hopefully the bad guys will be apprehended before we leave. Old Chief Rivers and Johnny Whitefeather are going to be working with a sketch artist today. Chief George saw the car a couple of days ago, and he saw the guys riding in it. He said he'd never seen them before, but he got a pretty good look."

"The old chief's very elderly, but he's sharp as a tack, and I'd believe what he says over most people. Well, I wish you every blessing and success today, and I hope old Chief George is successful in identifying those monsters. Just be careful."

"We'll be fine," said Paul. "Deputy Sheriff Wolf is going with us, along with Detective Brannigan and the professor, and they're licensed to carry a gun, so we'll have lots of protection."

"Well, I'll pray that God goes with you," said Andy as he bade them goodbye.

They pulled into the campground at 8:50 a.m. sharp. The detective and the professor were ready to go. Wolf arrived a few minutes later and was introduced to the family. He said they'd received the results of the fingerprints, and one of the perpetrators, Stanley Bowden, was well known by the police. The other one was not on the books.

Candace had already arrived and was chatting with the other women. Susan and Heather were ready to go, and Magen was delighted that she'd be riding with Candace.

"Okay, folks, we're ready to go," said Wolf. "We'll ride two by two, so stay in that format on the highway."

In fifteen minutes they were coming into Frank. Susan, Heather, and Magen gasped in horror when they saw the destruction the slide had caused. It's hard to imagine what a town that was three quarters buried would look like unless you saw it for yourself. No words can describe it. You had to feel it, to be overwhelmed by it, to get the picture. It was like the end of the world. They all felt a sorrow come over them, and they mourned the loss of the souls buried there, even though they didn't know them and weren't related in any way. As they stood there and looked out over the humongous rocks, they felt like they were there watching it happen.

David and Gordon gently told the ladies to get back on the bikes, and as they moved forward to climb the foothills of the Mountain that Moves, the ladies snuggled close to their partners and took comfort in their closeness. The group became very quiet as they pondered that, for the villagers, it really was the end of the world.

Wolf led the group slowly up the side of the mountain, and soon he was turning into the lane to his grandfather's cabin. Candace had phoned to let the old chief know they were coming. Wolf probably did as well. Anyway, there he was standing on the porch with his friend, Johnny, waiting to welcome them. He had a grin on his face a mile wide. There was no doubting that he was delighted to see them. Like he said, he loved a party, and to have so many people coming to see him gave him the chance to tell his stories.

"Hi, Miss Candy," he greeted Candace, and his grin got even wider. "I see you brought me a whole bunch of visitors. It's not my birthday till next month, but I love any excuse for a party. So what's the occasion?"

"Well, my friends heard you had the eyesight of an eagle, and they wondered if you could describe the little red car and its occupants that you saw driving by a couple of days ago. As you describe them, I'll try to sketch a picture to give to the police to help them identify the bad guys. I also told my friends about your wonderful teas, and Holly brought her mom to have tea with you."

Susan smiled and stepped forward. "Hi, Chief George. I'm Susan, Holly's mom. I brought something sweet for you to have with your tea," she said as she handed him the bag of goodies.

"Mighty kind of you, Miss Susan. Candy told you all about my sweet tooth, didn't she?" He grinned his toothless grin at the joke and giggled with delight. "Candy told me you were coming, so I put the kettle on. It should be boiling now. The tea won't be long. How many of you would like a cup?"

Eleven hands went up. Holly and Bonnie had bragged so much about the teas that they all wanted to try them.

"Do you mind if we stay outside, Chief?" said Candace. "I need the light to sketch, and you'll probably recall more, since that's where you were when you saw the car. Johnny could maybe help as well, since he was with you. I also brought you a sweet treat, so we'll just leave it here on the picnic table."

"Thanks, Candy. You never forget. Yeah, we can sit here. I'll be right back. Johnny, you can help me bring out the cups and honey."

Johnny and the old chief hurried inside the cabin. Holly and Bonnie ran after them to offer their help. It wasn't easy to keep up with these two. The kettle was boiling, and old Chief George reached up into the cupboard and brought down a beautiful, large, home crafted teapot. Holly wondered if one of his daughters or granddaughters had made it. He made the tea, setting it on the low heat to brew, and he moved around the kitchen like he was forty years younger, setting the cups and spoons out and the paper plates for the sweets. It was obvious he loved company.

Johnny carried the tray of cups and honey out to the picnic table, and Holly and Bonnie took care of the paper plates and utensils. Candace commandeered a corner of the table for her sketching materials. The old chief came to the door of the cabin and waved.

"Just a couple more minutes," he said. "Tea's almost ready."

The men were all standing together, discussing the case.

"We'll take a trip up to the mine and talk to the guards," said Wolf. "They didn't report anything yet, but I still want to take a look around. We didn't do that yesterday, because Susannah was our first priority. They might come back ... then again, they might not. It depends on how safe they feel up here."

"Tea's ready," the old chief shouted. Holly was carrying the tea-pot.

"Oh, it's really heavy. Paul, come and help me."

Paul ran to her immediately and took the pot. "You're right, this is heavy." He set it on the table. Wolf came over and picked it up.

"I'll pour," he said. "This pot's too heavy for Grandfather. My daughter made this for her great grandfather, because he has so many visitors his other teapot isn't big enough."

"I'm amazed at the talents of your people," said Heather. "This pot is exquisite. Have you ever thought of starting up a business, Chief, with your teas and your great granddaughter's teapots and biscuits?"

"Great granddaughter has a little shop in Frank. The tourists really like her art work. I'm too old to start a business. Great granddaughter's name is Star. She sends people out to have tea with me."

"This tea is like nectar of the gods," said Susan. "I must have the recipe. Are all the ingredients growing wild in the bush, Chief?"

"That's right. I promised young Holly I'd give you the recipe, so I got Star to type it out for you. I'll give it to you before you leave. Honey is what I use to sweeten it. It's all natural," he said.

Candace started asking old Chief George questions about the red car and its occupants, and as she and the chief talked, she started sketching. The others remained silent as they listened and watched the magic strokes of the pencil. Soon two faces appeared on the sketch pad. They didn't look like monsters, but Johnny said they looked exactly like them. That was good enough for Wolf.

Just then, Wolf's phone rang. He listened for a couple of minutes then snapped his phone closed and told everybody they had to clear the table off immediately.

"You have to go inside. The car's been spotted turning off onto the mountain trail. They're heading this way. I'd like the men to follow me to the mine. Holly's team can come if they want to, but the girls will have to hide in the bushes and be very quiet."

"Bonnie and I would like to go with our team," said Holly.

"Me too," said Peggy and Lorrie.

"We'll hide like we did before," said Peggy.

"Okay," said Wolf. "I guess that's only fair. You were in on it from the beginning, but you have to do what I tell you and stay hidden."

"We will," they all chimed in at once.

"If we leave immediately, we'll arrive ten minutes ahead of them. The car won't travel as well as the bikes, so let's go."

The table was cleared off like magic, and the others went into the cabin to await the outcome. The troupe mounted their bikes and peeled out of there, following Wolf as their leader as they headed for the mine. Wolf phoned the guards while riding to give them a heads-up.

The guards met them as they pulled in. Once the bikes were hidden, Wolf laid out his plan, and then they all burrowed into their hiding places to wait for the kidnappers to arrive. Everyone was on high alert, waiting to see what would happen. The car pulled up to the entrance and stopped. Two men got out. One was carrying a baseball bat.

The two men looked around and started towards the entrance. "Don't hit her anymore," said the one guy. "You'll kill her if you do."

"And what do you suggest we do to make her sign," said the guy with the bat. "We can't keep the car if she won't sign it over. We'll be stopped on the road and we'll go to jail—and I have no intention of going to jail. Anyway, whether or not she signs, we can't let her go. She can ID us."

"Then what are you planning to do?"

"If she doesn't sign, we'll block up the door to the mine," said the guy with the bat.

"Well, I'm not going in with you," said the one who was dragging his feet. "I can't watch you beating her, and I don't want to be part of this anymore. I won't take part in murder. Besides, I get claustrophobic in there."

"Maybe I should use the bat on you," said bat guy. "Well, you stay here if you want to. I'm not wasting any more time. I'm going in. If she wants me to stop hitting her, she'd better sign."

He stomped into the entrance and then seemed to remember that was a bad idea. He sucked in his breath and stepped more carefully. When he was out of sight, Wolf turned to the guards and signalled to them to pick up the nervous guy, who'd sat down on a rock and placed his elbows on his knees, dropping his head into his hands. He looked pretty desperate. The guards moved as stealthily as cats and had him gagged and handcuffed before he even knew what was happening. They dragged him into the bushes beside Wolf, who signalled to him to be quiet. His eyes were wide with fright, but he nodded his head to show he would behave and settled back quietly beside Wolf.

Suddenly, there was a roar from inside the mine, and the bat guy came running out. He looked around for his partner. When he didn't see him, he started screaming and cursing. "Stop playing around, numbskull. She's not here. Either she got away, or she went further into the mine. Where did you go, idiot? We have to go look for her!" He threw the bat on the ground and stomped his feet in rage.

He picked up the bat again and banged it over and over on the ground. The guards slipped up behind him. He was completely unaware of them and equally unaware that his temper tantrum was being viewed by an audience of nine people. Before he realized they were there, the guards threw a net over his head and tied him up like a chicken.

He screamed and kicked and cursed, but the more he kicked, the more entangled he became. When he realized he was surrounded by applauding young adults and lawmen, he stopped kicking. The look of surprise on his face would have been comical if the situation hadn't been so serious.

When his co-conspirator was hauled out in front of him, he knew he was done for. Just then, Sheriff Sky Rivers and Officers Cliff and Roland arrived in police cruisers. Wolf filled them in on what had transpired, and the two scoundrels were shoved separately and unceremoniously into the backs of the two cruisers. Roland would drive Susannah's car.

Surprisingly, the car didn't seem to have suffered any damage in the exchange. It even looked clean, but there were some stolen items in the trunk that would have to be sorted out and returned to their owners.

Holly bowed her head and said a quick prayer. "Thank you, Lord. Susannah will finally get some justice. Please help her to heal quickly and relieve her pain. Amen"

"Yes," said Bonnie, "but it's going to take a long time before she's able to live a normal life."

"True," said the professor, "but one thing she has going for her is the fact she's a swimmer. That's the best exercise there is to recover from injuries like the ones she's suffering from."

"I think we should stop and see her on the way back. It's just after noon, and we have to be at the lake at two, so we have time to spend a few minutes with Susannah. I hope she's awake so we can tell her we caught the kidnappers and got her car back. It might cheer her up a little. She needs some good news right now."

They stopped at the old chief's cabin to give them an update and pick up the rest of their group. Candace's sketch was a perfect image of the bad guys. Old Chief George invited them to come out any time. Susan was happy, because she had the recipe for the most heavenly tea she had ever tasted.

When they arrived at the hospital, they were told that Susannah was awake, but she was in a lot of pain. The nurse took them to her room.

"Please don't stay too long. Just a few minutes, and only two at a time," she warned.

Holly and Paul went in first as before. The pale, wan face that turned to them broke into a tentative smile as the nurse explained to her these were some of the people who'd rescued her the day before.

"I'm Holly Brannigan," said Holly, "and this is Paul Castles. We wanted to see how you were coming along."

"Thank you," she said. "I would have died if you hadn't found me."

"We found the kidnappers today," said Holly, "and we found your car. The kidnappers have been arrested, and your car is in terrific shape. At least they didn't damage it. I'm sorry they damaged you like they did. They're in jail and won't be able to hurt anyone else."

"Only one of the guys hurt me," Susannah said. "The other one kept trying to get him to stop, but without success. I think he was just as afraid of him as I was."

"I got that impression too," said Holly.

"I'm glad you're on the mend," said Paul. "Some of the rest of our search and rescue team are waiting to come in to see you, but if you're too tired, we'll tell them not to come till tomorrow."

"No, please tell them to come in. I want to thank them all. I can sleep later. Do you live around here?"

"No, we're from B.C., Vancouver area," said Paul. "We're teaching your class to swim, so don't worry about them. We're scuba divers."

"Yes," said Holly. "We'd like to keep in touch and invite you to come for a visit. You can recuperate at my house in Lions Bay. We have a scuba diving club, and we'll teach you to scuba dive if you like. Swimming will help you to recuperate."

"Thank you. I might take you up on that."

"We'd better go," said Holly, "and give the others a chance to see you. The nurse said we should only stay a few minutes, so we don't want to overdo it."

"Thank you again, Holly and Paul. I do hope we stay in touch."

Bonnie and Ted went in next, and Holly and Paul filled Peggy and Lorrie in on their visit.

"She'll probably be in hospital a long time," said Peggy. "We live here, so we'll visit her every day till she leaves the hospital, and we'll let you know how she's doing. Maybe we can help her with her rehab. We'll check with the physios."

"Oh, that would be super," said Holly. "I feel bad that we have to leave her on Sunday."

Ted and Bonnie came out of the hospital room, and Peggy and Lorrie took their turn. The teammates shared their experience, and they all wished they could be there to help Susannah along, but they had a good feeling that Peggy and Lorrie would be great as their stand-ins. While they were waiting for Peggy and Lorrie, they all had protein bars, of which Holly always seemed to have an endless supply. She set two aside for the other two girls.

"We won't have time to eat before the class, so these will do until we're finished. What do you say we go for pizza after class? I suddenly have a craving for pizza. Peggy and Lorrie will know the best place in the Pass."

"Yeah!" It was unanimous.

When Peggy and Lorrie joined them, Holly asked where the best pizza place was in the Pass. They both answered at once, "Gepetto's."

When they arrived at the lake, Charlie and Sally were already there. Andy, as usual, wanted to feed them. He was excited to hear about the capture of the thieving kidnappers, so the team brought him up-to-date. They had some hot chocolate and hotdogs, more or less to make Andy happy. He just wanted to do something for them. Since they wouldn't be swimming, but just standing in the water instructing, they decided to have some.

The kids were excited to get going. They'd been practicing in the shallow water and wanted to show their instructors what they could do. At two o'clock sharp, Ted chased them all into the water and told them to find their instructors. Sam had joined them again, even though he'd been swimming in the river with Willie. It was a big surprise when Cliff showed up.

"I thought you were working this afternoon," Holly said.

"I was, but Roland said he could manage without me, so I booked off for an hour. I wanted at least one more lesson."

"That's good," said Paul, "because I want to show you how to rescue someone and bring them out of the water."

"Do you think I'm ready for that?"

"Not yet," said Paul, "but I'll show you how, and you can practice till you get it right."

"Okay. What do I do first?"

"You need to learn to swim on your back. You lie on your back and use your arms like oars. Like this." He showed him. "Right arm back and swing it forward like you did in the crawl, except you're reaching back behind you instead of forward. Then the left … reach back and swing forward. Practice this until you feel confident before you try to rescue anyone.

"If the right arm is the strongest, that's the one you'll use for swimming in a rescue. Grasp the drowning victim under the chin with the other hand, and pull him up against you on his back, like this. Reach back and over with the right arm and pull the water like an oar, and kick as hard as you can."

"Who's going to take a chance on letting me practice with them in the water?" asked Cliff.

"If you can borrow a demonstration dummy from the fire department, that would work," Paul suggested.

"Good idea," Cliff agreed. "I went for a swim last night and again early this morning. I'm really stoked at how much I've learned in a few days."

"Okay, let's see what you can do. Take a deep breath and just lie back flat in the water. Reach straight out with your arms and you'll float, like this." He demonstrated. "Do it like that, and I guarantee you won't sink."

Cliff followed Paul's directions and was surprised that he really was floating. It was obvious he trusted Paul when he said he wouldn't sink. Ted was tied up with a couple of other kids, so Sam and Willie had been watching and listening to Paul's directions to Cliff. They decided to give it a try. Even though Sam had been more scared than Willie in the water, he believed everything Paul said, and he lay back in the water like he was going to take a nap and floated like a raft.

"I can't believe this," he said. "I'm just lying here in the water, and I'm not sinking. Hey, Ted, look at Willie and me," he shouted when Ted joined them. "We're floating!"

"Super cool, Sam," said Ted. "I guess you don't need me anymore," he joked. "Okay, let's see you swim backwards. Reach back with your right arm and use it like an oar to pull it through the water. Now do the same with the left. While you're doing this, kick in a scissors kick with your feet. That's it! You'll be awkward at first, but keep practicing, and you'll get the hang of it."

Cliff was determined to master this exercise. He felt it was important for his job to be able to rescue anyone, child or adult, if they were in trouble in the water. He found it hard to remember to kick while he was using his arms, but he did the best he could, and when he concentrated, it began to come together.

"Don't forget to breathe," said Paul. "You're doing super! Keep it up and try to coordinate your feet with your arms and breathing. You can practice this exercise in your beds till you get the rhythm."

Holly and the other instructors were taking their lead from Paul and had been introducing the backstroke to their teams. The kids all soaked it up like little sponges. It was amazing how fast they learned, and they didn't have the fear that adults all seem to have. They just watched and learned.

"Ted, would you show us how you saved Dad?" asked Willie.

"Well, I won't show you how to dive down ten feet, because I don't want you trying that yet. That will come with experience when you learn to dive, but I'll show you how I saved a drowning man and pulled Sam through the water to the boat … if Paul wouldn't mind me using him for the demonstration. This is the exercise you need to learn to save a life. I'll wait for Paul to swim out about sixty feet. He'll thrash around in the water and start to sink like a drowning man," said Ted. "Then I'll show you how to save him."

They were all watching now. When he went into his drowning act, Paul seemed like someone who couldn't swim a stroke and was in danger of drowning. He sank and disappeared twice, only to bounce up again. Ted tore like a streak of lightning across the water to the so-called victim.

Paul was going down for the third time when Ted dove under and came up behind him, grabbing him firmly under the chin and kicking wildly for the surface. Paul pretended to be unconscious, and Ted did the backstroke with one arm while dragging Paul by the chin with the other. Paul didn't move a muscle. He certainly seemed incapacitated. It was an amazing show of bravery.

The adults and kids all applauded the demonstration. Andy and the parents were watching from the bank and were super impressed.

"I think we should have been taking those lessons," said one of the parents. "I can't swim a stroke. My kid would have to save me."

"Those young people are miracle workers," said Andy. "I don't know what we'd have done without them this week. They saved Susannah and found her car, and they caught the kidnappers. They also found the things that were stolen, and they taught the kids how to swim. Even Cliff learned to swim."

Celebration

CHAPTER 12

THE YOUNG SWIMMING INSTRUCTORS ALL DECIDED TO JOIN THEIR PARENTS IN the Blairmore camp for dinner. Holly told Andy they would have a one hour class the following morning at 10:00 a.m. to give the kids a good basic knowledge in swimming. The team would probably spend the rest of the day exploring.

The children had all promised they would stay in the shallow end, no deeper than their chests, until they could swim like Paul and Ted, and to only swim when an adult was watching them. The adults wouldn't drown if they had to go in after any one of them at that depth, even if they couldn't swim. Holly told Andy she didn't know if they were leaving on Saturday or Sunday. It would depend on their parents, but she promised they would give them a concert the following night.

"Tell the kids to make a list of their favourite songs and choruses," said Ted, "and we'll make a list of our favourite songs. Do you mind if we invite our parents to the concert? Some of them also play instruments."

"Invite anyone you like. We don't often get entertainment here. We'll plan on having it in the hall in case it rains. It'll be more comfortable for the ladies, and we'll have a light reception with tea, coffee, hot chocolate, and pop. Thank you for all you've done for us. We'll invite a few people from town as well. It should be a great way to end the week."

Peggy drove her car into town. She loaded up the instruments, along with those divers who didn't have a bike. The parents were happily surprised when the group arrived.

"How nice that you decided to join us," Susan said. "You've been so busy on search and rescue, I thought we probably wouldn't see you again till we were packing up to leave."

"Well, Mom, you know we can't stay away too long from your cooking," said Holly. "We're taking a break so we can socialize a little bit. Who won the golf tournament?"

"You know doctors spend lots of time on the golf course," said Susan, so Molly and Robert's team won."

"Congratulations, Aunt Molly and Uncle Robert," said Peggy.

"Well, I think I should mention that for somebody who never played golf before," said the professor, "Heather has a monster swing. She hit that ball so hard, it's probably in the next county, never to be seen again."

"Oh, I probably didn't hit it that far," she said. "You just didn't want to go after it."

"You hit the ball," he said. "You're supposed to go after it."

"Well, that doesn't sound fair," she pouted. "I gave it a good wallop. You're my side-kick, and you're supposed to find it."

Everybody laughed hysterically at this repartee.

"Making up your own rules again, are you, Mom?" Ted was laughing just as hard as everybody else. "By the way, you're all invited to a concert at the lake tomorrow at 6:00 p.m. Bring your instruments and talent with you. There'll be refreshments served."

"Yes," said Paul, "Andy is so thankful that we found Susannah and the stolen goods and taught the kids to swim that I think he'd like to keep us here. He said God sent us."

"Perhaps He did," said Heather. "You're a pretty marvellous group of kids. Just think what would've happened to that girl if you hadn't found her."

"We're pretty happy we found her," said Holly. "Of course, we have to give some of the credit to old Chief George and his grandson, Wolf … and to all the people who volunteered to search. Without their help and suggestions, we might not have found her. It's difficult when you're searching through unfamiliar territory."

"This is beautiful countryside," said Ted. "We're going to do some exploring and scuba diving tomorrow now that we've found Susannah and the kidnappers. I hope those guys get the book thrown at them."

"I was talking to Cliff," said David. "He said that one of the kidnappers, named Billy Donnelly, is singing like a bird. He said Stanley Bowden talked him into going along with him to steal a bike and some small stuff, and then he talked him into going after the canoes. They're scuba divers, and Bowden has a nasty temper. Donnelly tried to talk him out of stealing the car and hurting the girl. He refused to hurt the girl, and Bowden threatened him when he tried to leave, and said he would use the bat on him."

"Yes, we heard him threatening to use the bat on him at the mine when Donnelly refused to go in with him. Susannah told us at the hospital that only one of the kidnappers beat her, and the other one tried to stop him."

"That might help Donnelly at his trial," said David. He was talking as a lawyer now. "Bowden is looking at thirty years to life. Donnelly may have a reduced sentence because he's cooperating and because he was threatened. He didn't take part in the beatings, but he'll probably get ten to fifteen years."

"I'm just thankful we were here and able to help," said Holly.

"I worry about you a lot," said Susan. "I sometimes forget you're eighteen and an adult. You're very responsible, and you care so much about other people. You and your team save people from some of the worst situations we can imagine. I'm so proud of you and your friends."

"I agree," said Heather. "I'm glad Ted found Holly's team. They're great together, and I wouldn't have found my future husband without them," she said with a twinkle in her eyes.

"Right on, Heather," said the professor. "They rescued me from bachelorhood. Search and rescue seems to be their motto."

"No, it's not really. 'Underwater Ventures' is our motto. Search and rescue just seems to go along with it," said Holly.

"Okay, everybody," said Susan. "Gather around the table. Dinner is ready. Heather, Kim, and Kate can help me bring the food out of the motorhome. The table is all set. Holly, you can bring the condiments and buns, and Bonnie the salt and pepper and butter and cream. They're all laid out on the counters and tables in the motorhome. I love it when we have so much help. Everything comes together so quickly."

She was right. With so much help and everybody doing their job, the food was on the table in a few minutes. Heather always got into a giggle when she looked around the table at all the redheads. No one would deny the fact they were a family, because they all looked alike.

Lynda and Jeremiah's children, Joanne and Kitty, and Kim, Lynda, and Molly had hair like spun gold. Among all the children, there was only one dark haired one in the lot, and that was Willie. When Holly remarked on it, she was told that Willie was adopted. Magen was so much older than Willie, and when Kim was told she wouldn't be able to have another child, she and Jeremiah decided to adopt a boy, so they got Willie.

"Yeah!" said Willie. "I'm a lucky boy. I've got the best parents in the world, and a really cool sister."

Phil was asked to say grace, and they bowed their heads. "Dear Heavenly Father," he said. "Thank you for bringing our family together, and may this day be a celebration of thanks for helping us to rescue Susannah from the brutal beatings she endured for the past four days. We ask for healing mercies for this brave young girl, and that you will ease her pain and help her to make a quick recovery. We also ask your blessing on the food we are about to receive; bless it to our bodies, and bless the hands that prepared it and us in thy service. In Jesus' name, amen."

Heather was still amused by all the redheads. "We must get pictures of all the sun gods and goddesses at this table," Heather said. "Thank goodness I brought my camera. No one would ever believe this if I didn't prove it with a picture. It's like a golden halo from the sun captured in one spot. Please excuse me, I'm just going to get my camera." She left the table and was back in a flash. "Don't pay any attention to me, folks. This will only take a couple of minutes." She skipped around the table, trying to get everybody into the shot.

"Please sit down, Heather, and have your dinner," said Gordon. "You can do that after we've finished."

"No, this is probably the only time I'll be able to get you all together. Okay, I've got you all in the shot. Smile everybody." They all smiled, some with food in their mouths, and some with their forks raised with food half way to their mouths. Heather was delighted and clicked once more in case the other one didn't turn out. Now she could eat.

The table was groaning with food. It was like a banquet. You'd never believe it was served in a campground, at least not unless you knew Susan and her way with food.

"Eat up, guys," said Holly. "There are going to be some great leftovers for tomorrow. Don't let me forget to fill my duffle bag."

Bonnie and the guys laughed. "As if you'd ever forget," said Bonnie.

The dessert was English trifle loaded with whipped cream and strawberries. There were collective moans of pleasure from everyone as they ate the delicious delicacy. Susan was in her element.

"Pure ambrosia," said Kate. "You must give me the recipe."

"Of course," said Susan. "And now I have a surprise for you all."

"I thought we'd just had it," said Molly. "This dinner was superb."

"Oh, well this is something new," Susan told her. "We're going to have some of old Chief George's special tea. I've never tasted anything like it."

As she spoke, she was pouring. "You take it with honey, and the honey is on the table, so help yourselves and enjoy."

As with the dessert, when they all took their first sips of the tea, there were collective sighs of "Ohs," "Wows," and "Ahs." Kate called it nectar of the gods.

"Can you buy this tea?" Kate asked. "Does the old chief sell it?"

"I don't think so," said Susan, "but if you go to visit him and listen to his stories, your reward is a cup of his tea. You might even get a second cup. It depends on how long you'll stay and listen to his stories. He has other teas also, all his own special blends, and the ingredients are all from nature's own wilderness garden. He should have a tea room in town and sell the teas with his granddaughter's scrumptious biscuits. I think he'd have an audience every day to listen to his stories."

"I certainly would drop in every day for a cup of this tea," said Kate.

"Perhaps you can talk him into it," said Holly. "Offer to go into business with him, keeping in mind he'll be 102 next month. Well, I think we should go," said Holly. "We should take advantage of the fact that our rescue mission is completed. The weather is glorious, and we should do what we came here to do. Let's go scuba diving this evening."

The rest of her teammates and the diving cousins all agreed, so they thanked Susan, praising her culinary skills, and left for the lake. They took the time to tidy up their tents and equipment and to give their dinner time to settle before heading into the water.

The little kids watched wide-eyed as the divers walked into the water in their scuba diving equipment looking like the cast of *Star Wars*. They watched until the divers disappeared into the depths and made their way towards the wreck of the railway cars. The underwater flora was beautiful, and just as they were about to cross to the left side of the lake, they saw another wreck.

It was an old car—a sedan. They wondered what the story was about this wreck. How did it get out so far into the lake? Perhaps Andy could tell them. It was an interesting mystery. Holly decided she'd better start a journal.

When they reached the wrecks of the railway cars, they took pictures with their underwater cameras. After what they'd seen in the past few days in the town of Frank, and the damage that was done to a sweet girl like Susannah by a beast of a man as monstrous as a terrorist, they were more able to accept the train wreck as an accident that was probably no one's fault. They would sleep better tonight and would be able to sleep in the next day.

The following day, Andy told them the story he'd heard about the car.

"It was about seventy-five years ago when it happened," he said. "The driver and passengers were coming home from a dance in Sparwood. It had been snowing for about three days, and people were warned to stay off the road, but these people didn't listen. They went to the dance anyway. They didn't have the roads we have today. The snow turned into a blizzard, and the road was blocked, so nothing was moving.

"Some of the men in the car had to get back to work at the mine, so they decided to drive across the frozen lake. They pushed the car and slid it down the bank onto the ice. Fishermen had been out on the lake in ice tents, and they'd driven their cars onto the ice and found it was okay because they were close to the edge. They didn't go near the middle.

"But these guys took their car farther out, and the ice wasn't thick enough because of the currents, so they went through. They all managed to climb out onto the ice before the car sank out of sight. That's the story I heard. I don't think anybody drowned. The ice was thick enough for them to walk on, but not for a car loaded with people."

"Is there a record of the accident?" Ted asked.

"I don't know," said Andy. "In those days, they would have just put that down to drinking and stupidity. Nobody would be so foolish as to try that today. And also, the roads are really good now."

"Wow! That must have been cold," said Bonnie. "Did anybody have to be pulled out of the water?"

"I don't know. You could probably google it on the Internet and get the proper story. I think it made the newspapers."

It rained some during the night, but by the time the young divers woke up in the morning, the sun was out and everything smelled fresh and clean. They'd promised the kids another practice lesson, so they were free until ten o'clock. Holly set out their breakfast. The duffle bag was full of leftovers from the previous evening's dinner, compliments of her mother, and she laid out a mouth-watering feast for the meal.

Socrates had made himself at home. He strutted around like he was the king, and the kids loved him. Holly felt bad that they would have to take him with them when they left.

The practice lesson went great. All the kids were swimming, some better than others, but practice would take care of the slower ones. Sam and Cliff were elated that they were swimming as well as they were, and they promised Paul and Ted that they would practice every day.

The rest of the day was spent diving and exploring. Around four o'clock they went to see Susannah at the hospital, and they were surprised at how her recuperation was coming along. They met her parents and received many hugs of thanks along with tears of joy that they still had their daughter. They all promised to keep in touch and wrote down phone numbers, mailing, and email addresses.

The kids had a concert to perform at six o'clock, so they had to say goodbye. The girls wiped the tears in their eyes as they were leaving.

"Thank you, all," said Susannah. "I'll never forget you. We'll be friends forever."

"And remember my open invitation for you to come to the coast," said Holly. "We'll be looking forward to seeing you again. Okay, guys," she said. "It's time to go. We have very little time to prepare." And they were off.

When they got to the lake, they discovered Andy and his staff had everything ready. The chairs were all set up in the hall facing the stage. Four long tables covered with white tablecloths were placed along the far wall. They were loaded with refreshments such as sandwiches, dipping vegetables, pickles, fruit, chips, and cakes. There was also coffee, tea, juice, and pop.

Holly and her group were choosing choruses for the kids and songs for their group. Holly made a list, and Bonnie ran up and down the keyboard as she picked out the intro for each song.

"I wish I'd brought my violin," said Ted. "I was afraid I'd damage it on the trip. I'd like to ask Mom to sing "The Holy City," but that song needs a violin."

Andy happened to hear him. "You need a violin?" he asked. "We have one here. It hasn't been played since my Uncle Tommy passed away. I'd sure like to hear it again. Hey, Danny, bring Uncle Tommy's violin out here. Ted's going to play it."

When Ted lifted the violin out of the case, he gazed at it in awe as he ran his hand reverently over the beautiful finish of the wood. He was speechless and uttered a silent, "Wow!" Picking up the bow, he closed his eyes and ran it over the strings. The sound made you think of angels.

Ted spent the next few minutes tuning the instrument and treating the bow with the rosin he found in the case, and then he began to play "Danny Boy." The staff all came running to listen. The old violin sounded like a Stradivarius, and Andy had tears in his eyes as he stood with his hands clasped like he was in prayer.

When Ted finished the melody, everybody applauded. Just then, the visitors began to arrive. Andy knew everybody. Some were the volunteers who helped in the search and rescue. Andy had put the word out to Milton to make sure they were included. Cliff and Roland arrived around the same time as Wolf and Sky, who accompanied his father, old Chief George, and his friend, Johnny Whitefeather.

When Holly's parents arrived accompanied by the professor and Heather and all his relatives, the hall was already pretty full. Some of them were carrying guitars. Phil had his banjo. A section was roped off and reserved for them, and another up front for the children from the swimming class. The children's parents were seated in the row behind them. Willie joined the little kids. A special area was reserved for the volunteers who had taken part in the search. Andy was really excited, as they hadn't had a concert since his Uncle Tommy passed away.

At six o'clock sharp, the young performers were on stage and ready to play. Andy took over the mic to introduce them.

"Hi, folks! Welcome to an evening you're not likely to ever forget. We're so fortunate to have these nine young people here tonight. Ted Lumley will MC, and he'll introduce his friends who have kindly offered to entertain us. Before we start the main part of the concert, we're going to sing some songs and choruses with the children. The kids chose these songs. They made a list, and I'm sure most of you will know them. I'll turn this over to Ted."

"Hi there, everybody. Let me introduce you to our keyboard player, Bonnie Tilson." Bonnie raised her hand in greeting. "On guitars, we have Paul Castles and twin sisters Peggy and Lorrie Clayborn." They too raised their hands. "And Holly Brannigan, who plays the piano accordion." Holly waved and hit a key on her instrument. "And I sometimes play the violin. Okay, kids. Let's start out with little Pricilla's favourite, 'This Little Light of Mine.'"

Bonnie and Holly gave an intro, and the others strummed on their guitars. The kids sang like little angels and jumped immediately into "There Is a Happy Land."

"Great singing, kids," said Ted. "How about a song that every kid's mom sings to them to let them know they love them? How many of you know 'You Are My Sunshine'?" Every hand went up. They sang it with smiles on their faces, and the audience joined in. Then they swung into 'Jacob's Ladder' and 'Jesus Loves Me.' They sang non-stop for another fifteen minutes.

"It's time now for us to sing your moms' and dads' favourites," said Ted, "so we'll take a little break and let Mr. Andy talk."

"Thanks, Ted," said Andy. "Most of you know about the trouble we had here at the lake this week, but for those of you who don't know, the young people on stage tonight bailed us out in more ways than one.

"They came here for a vacation just to scuba dive and explore and to visit family, and they arrived at the camp on the morning after our swimming coach, Susanna, went missing. Since we're right by the lake, they decided they'd like to stay here to scuba dive and explore underwater and in the cave. But when they discovered Susannah was missing, they decided to fill in for her and teach the kids themselves. They were experienced in search and rescue at the coast, so they decided to go in search of Susannah.

"The robbers had been thieving all through the Pass, and they stole some items from the camp, including canoes, bikes, generators, and a few other things. These young people organized a search party and spent their whole vacation searching for the scoundrels. They found them too, along with the stolen items.

"They also found Susannah tied up in one of the mines. She'd been beaten to within an inch of her life, and she's now recuperating in the hospital with broken bones and wounds that will take many months to mend. The doctors said she would have died if our young adventurers hadn't found her when they did.

"I believe there are angels on the earth, and I believe God intervened and sent these young folk to this camp, so let's give them a big welcome and show our appreciation for their love and care for strangers in need."

Everyone stood up. The applause rocked the building. There were even some whistles and cheers.

"And now, folks," said Andy, "I'll turn the mic over to Ted."

It took a couple of minutes for the applause to die down before Ted could speak. "Thank you, folks," he said. "We're so happy to be here, and

I thought you'd like to know that we saw Susannah this afternoon, and she's coming along great. She's looking forward to being able to swim again and visiting us at the coast. We'd like to start off this evening with a song for Susannah—'Thank You, Lord, for Saving My Soul.'"

Everyone seemed to know that chorus. It was so appropriate.

"We'd like to show our admiration for this beautiful part of our country, so our next song will be 'The Blue Canadian Rockies,' and I'd like to invite those of our family who have brought their instruments with them to join us on stage."

The band swung into the song while David, Phil, Gordon, Peggy, and Lorrie joined the group. As they arrived, they immediately started to play without missing a beat. Gordon was playing on the mouthorgan, and Ted led them in singing the song. Soon everyone in the hall was singing. The harmony was glorious. When the song was finished, Ted waved to his mother in the audience.

"That was great, folks. You're all good singers. Now I'd like to introduce you to my mother, Heather Lumley." He beckoned to her to join him on the stage. She made her way up beside Ted. "Mom is a classical music teacher," he said. "She organizes and directs at least three musicals a year. That's how I met my friends, Holly and Paul, and my beautiful girlfriend, Bonnie. We appeared in one of Mom's musicals together.

"I'd like to invite my mom to sing a wonderful song called 'The Holy City,' as only my mother can sing it. Bonnie, Holly, and I will accompany her."

The other musicians stepped back as Heather stepped up to the mic, and the girls began the intro. Ted joined his mother on the violin as she began to sing. This was the first time Gordon had heard her sing in public. He stood there entranced as her beautiful classical voice soared to the rafters. Ted's rendition on the violin was enchanting.

There wasn't a sound in the hall. Even the children seemed to be in a trance. Ted played like a virtuoso, skillfully controlling the sound to complement Heather's voice. When the song ended, the audience stood to give her a standing ovation. Heather bowed and was about to go and sit down, but the audience wouldn't let her. They kept applauding and shouting for more, so Ted whispered to her, and she nodded yes. He spoke to the girls, and they played the intro to "Danny Boy."

Ted played the first verse and chorus as a solo. Most of the audience closed their eyes to listen. Then Heather began to sing. It was like a lullaby that curled around your heart. You could hear the sadness of a mother singing goodbye to her son. One man whispered to his wife: "What a voice! I feel like I'm there." Danny had tears in his eyes. The applause burst forth with another standing ovation, and when the audience sat down, Ted asked his mother to stay on stage with them.

The concert went on for almost an hour and a half. They sang a mixture of country songs and familiar hymns. Then Holly stepped up to the mic, and Ted stepped back.

"We'd like to end this concert with a surprise for you. Ted's mom isn't the only classical singer in their family. We've been blessed to not only have him as our friend and as a scuba diving teammate, but also in our musical group. Ted has a voice that makes the angels sing and celebrate, and we'd like to hear him sing what is a very popular song today, 'Hallelujah.' Bonnie and I will accompany him."

Ted stepped up to the mic, and Holly stepped back to pick up her piano accordion. She and Bonnie played the intricate introduction, and Ted began to sing. Andy clasped his hands together as in prayer and closed his eyes as he had before. The audience listened, enraptured.

You could have heard a pin drop. Holly, Bonnie, and Heather came in with the "ahs," their harmonious voices rising to a crescendo as they soared higher. When the last note sounded, there was a brief lull and then a salvo of applause burst forth with everyone standing cheering and shouting, "Bravo, bravo." The band took their bows, and Andy stepped up to the mic. His smile was so wide he could hardly talk.

"Let's show our appreciation to our young visitors to thank them for this wonderful concert and for finding Susannah and the criminals."

The applause burst forth again, and when it had died down, Andy invited them all to stay for refreshments. The men got together and removed the chairs to set up folding tables. Each table seated eight.

The people lined up by the food tables and by the time they had their plates filled, twelve tables were all in place. Holly chose a table where her parents, the professor, Heather, and she and her teammates could sit. She sat between her father and Paul. Andy told them there were ninety-eight attendees. The place was full, but there was lots of food. Sheila kept bringing replacements out of the cooler. They had prepared for this crowd.

"Great performance, Pumpkin," Holly's dad said.

"I'm so happy everything went so well," said Holly. "Now I won't go home and worry about Susannah. She's in good hands. If we hadn't found her, I don't think I could have gone home until we did."

"That's good, because we decided to start back for home tomorrow, just in case something happens on the road. Remember on the way here there was a slide in Revelstoke. If we get stuck on the road, we want to have time to make arrangements. You never know in the mountains. I have appointments Monday, and you start at UBC on Tuesday."

Paul reached over and took her hand. "Your dad's right, Holly. This has been the best vacation. We've done everything we like to do. We've scuba-dived on two wrecks, explored a cave, saved Sam and Willie from drowning, searched for and rescued Susannah and saved her life, helped to catch the kidnappers and found the loot they stole, taught twenty kids and two adults how to swim, and gave a concert to ninety-eight people. All that in less than a week. What more do you want to do?"

"Wow! When you put it like that, I guess you're right." She reached over and gave him a hug. "You always set me straight when I wander. You're the best."

Just then the professor walked through the door, followed by a beautiful German Shepherd police dog. He walked over to Andy and handed him some papers.

"Sorry, I have to take Socrates home with me tomorrow, Andy, but I found a replacement for him. I'd like to introduce you to Einstein, a police dog with more medals for bravery than a four-star general."

"But how ..." said Andy. "How did you get a beautiful animal like that?" Einstein sat up straight and seemed to be listening to the conversation. "With all those medals, I doubt we could afford him. He must be worth a lot of money."

"He was, but he's been retired. Einstein is only five years old, but he got shot in the leg while chasing a suspect, so he had to be discharged. That earned him another medal for bravery, because even though he was injured, he stopped the suspect and held him till his partner was able to catch up and make the arrest. He's been living with an elderly retired police officer who passed away two weeks ago, and Einstein needs a new family to care for."

"He looks like a great dog," said Andy, "but what about the kids? We can't have him getting rough with the kids."

"Einstein loves kids. He's very gentle, and he'll protect them and everyone in this campground like it's his job. He only goes after bad guys, and only if he's ordered to by his partner. You're his new partner, and this notebook gives you the code words to use if you need him to help in any way. Learn them by heart, and either destroy it or put the notebook in a safe place. Einstein is yours now. Don't be afraid of him. You can pet him and make a friend of him."

Andy was ecstatic. "I've never had a dog," he said. He petted Einstein and was delighted when the dog put his nose into his hand and licked it. That's when he knew they'd be friends. Holly and Paul were making their way outside to go for a walk when they spotted the dog.

"What a beautiful dog!" Holly exclaimed.

"His name is Einstein," said Andy. "He's a decorated police dog, and Professor Clayborn gave him to me. I'm his new partner."

"Wow!" She petted and stroked the soft fur. "Hi there, Einstein," she said. "Take good care of our friends here, and keep all the bad guys away." The dog nuzzled up to her and licked her hands.

The sun was going down and twilight was setting in as Holly and Paul walked with their arms around each other along the edge of the lake. Bonnie and Ted were sitting snuggled together on the pier looking out over the water.

"What a terrific way to end a vacation," said Holly.

"Yes." Paul stopped and pulled Holly into a hug. "You are what makes the holiday terrific for me," he said.

"As you are for me, Paul."

She laid her head on his shoulder, and they snuggled side by side, their arms around each other's waist. They both gazed in awe out over the lake at the sunset's magic beams sparkling like fairy dust over the water. "Isn't this perfectly enchanting?" Holly whispered.

"Perfectly enchanting, just like you," Paul murmured, and he reached over and kissed her gently on the lips.

OTHER BOOKS BY KATHLEEN

Lyndaman Island Manor
ISBN 978-1-4866-1408-0

Lyndaman Island Manor is the fourth book in the Holly Brannigan Mystery series. Holly Brannigan and her three teenage friends, Paul Castles, Ted Lumley, and her best friend, Bonnie Tilson, find themselves in a dangerous situation when they visit Lyndaman Island Manor at the invitation of multi-billionaire Harvey Fields. They invite eight friends from their scuba diving club to come with them.

Strange things begin to happen after they arrive on the island, so Mr. Fields calls in Holly's father, a well known detective, to solve the case. Holly and her three friends had helped Detective Brannigan in the past when teenagers were the culprits. The four young sleuths were able to infiltrate teen groups to get information. There are dangers and threats at every turn on the island.

Donnymead Castle
ISBN 978-1-4866-0801-0

Follow the exciting adventures of teen amateur sleuth Holly Brannigan, the daughter of Detective David Brannigan.

When Holly and her family visit Holly's grandmother in her cottage on the grounds of Donnymead Castle, Holly is fascinated with the castle and manages to talk the caretaker into giving her a tour. But mysterious activity has been taking place on the castle grounds and Holly will have to put her sleuthing skills to the test.

Join Holly and her friend Tim on their explorations of the ancient village. Trace the threads of history from the past into the future and follow Holly and Tim as they discover that things aren't always as they appear. As the mystery deepens, Holly and Tim become lost in history, but can they discover who is behind the criminal activity in Donnymead?

Scuba Hijinks
ISBN 978-1-4866-0805-8
Scuba Hijinks is the second book in the "Holly Brannigan Mystery" series. Set on the West Coast of Canada in the Lions Bay and Porteau Bay area, the story follows the adventures of teen sleuth Holly Brannigan and her friends, Bonnie, Paul, and Ted as they team up with Holly's father, Detective David Brannigan, to catch a gang of rogue scuba divers. Holly and her friends learn to scuba dive in order to pursue the criminals, and they bravely face challenges and dangers throughout the case. Thrust into a world of kidnapping and vandalism, the amateur detectives use their new skills and unlimited trust in each other to bring the gang to justice.

Garibaldi Mountain
ISBN 978-1-4866-1124-9
Holly Brannigan and her three teenage friends–Paul Castles, Ted Lumley, and her best friend, Bonnie Tilson–have helped attorney David Brannigan on cases in the past, but this is the most dangerous mystery yet. A family with three children has disappeared, along with a close friend of the family, while camping in Garibaldi Provincial Park. When Holly and her friends hear of the disaster, they join a Mountain Search and Rescue team of volunteers. In very short order, Holly's team find clues that make them suspicious of foul play.

Follow Holly and her team as they search through torrential rain and fog, confront a dangerous wolf and its pack, and dodge men with bows and arrows who are terrorizing them as they race the clock to find the missing family. There are new threats and dangers at every turn!

A Holly Brannigan Mystery: Garibaldi Mountain is the third in the series.

All Roads Lead to Home
ISBN 978-1-4866-0789-1

Kathleen has discovered something magical in every province of this grand country, Canada. She sees the beauty in God's gifts to us: the mountains, the valleys, the trees, and the rivers and lakes, which have all inspired her poetry. Most poems are spiritual, some are for children, and some are just plain silly. Come and journey through the hills of Ireland, the cities of Ontario, and the majestic mountains of British Columbia with Kathleen's poetry. She hopes you find something to warm your heart.

Kathleen W. Forbes wrote her first poem when she was eight years old. The poems in this collection were written over the course of Kathleen's lifetime, and provide a small glimpse of her journey from childhood to the present day. As she changed over the years, so have her poems. In this way, they reflect the nature of life itself. Kathleen's father, also a poet and a pastor, once told her that he treasured her poems, which was the greatest accolade of all.

Camping at Blueberry Mountain
ISBN 978-1-4866-0797-6

An adventure is afoot in the town of Green Oaks as eight-year-old Penelope Henry gets the best surprise of her summer: a camping trip to beautiful Blueberry Mountain. The whole family, including her mama, papa, and brother Zinger, pack up their cart and head into the wilderness to relax, meet new lifelong friends, and learn valuable lessons that will forever change them.

But not everything about Blueberry Mountain is as peaceful as it seems. When a group of bandits start causing trouble in camp, it's up to Penny and her friends to save the day—with the help of an irreverent leprechaun named Dinty, who only appears to children.

Penelope Henry at the Circus
ISBN 978-1-4866-0793-8

Penelope's world turns upside-down with the arrival of the circus in her normally quiet village of Green Oaks. Just in case that's not exciting enough, it's also her ninth birthday!

When a monkey escapes from the circus and gets into a tangle with one of Penelope's friends, the circus owner invites them all to see the show—for free. All of Penelope's dreams come true when she is chosen to participate in one of the circus's most exciting acts.

But trouble strikes when the lions get out of their enclosure and the elephant trainer mysteriously goes missing, threatening the entire circus. Will the show be able to go on? With the help of Dinty the leprechaun, Penelope and her new friends are sure to have their hands full.

Penelope Henry at the Country Jamboree
ISBN 978-1-4866-1000-6

Country Jamboree will take you on a weekend of fun for the whole family. Join Penelope and her family and friends down on the farm for a rodeo with their country cousins where they'll watch the horse racing, the chuck wagons, and trick riding! Encounter mystery and discovery with surprises around every corner. Although facing danger and uncertainty, Penelope and friends are protected by Dinty Finnigan, the Irish leprechaun who protects small children and brings fun and magic everywhere he goes. Penelope and her friends will guide you on adventures great and small as they explore the farm and all the fun to be had!